He was mesmeriz shadows in the hig watched Hadleigh p ballet. Hidden under layers of feathers, she was almost unrecognizable, yet he was unable to take his eyes off her. He had come again to sit in the balcony, as if by watching from afar he could uncover the secret of this attraction. Once revealed, he could overcome it and go on about his business, and his life would remain uncomplicated. He hated having his life complicated. He'd had enough of that growing up, but managed to rid himself of that baggage (or so he hoped), and had gone on to establish a rewarding, although sometimes lonely, life for himself. Now this. This beautiful, shy lady had appeared and magically taken over his life, just like she did when she stepped on stage. He couldn't ignore her any more than he could have turned and walked out on her performance. Nor did he want to. But he knew he was opening the door to things better left alone.

Dancing in Time

by

Violet Rightmire

To
Heather
and
Janette
with best wishes
Violet Rightmire

Dancing in Time

Cover Art by *Tamra Westberry*

The Wild Rose Press
PO Box 708
Adams Basin, NY 14410-0706
Visit us at www.thewildrosepress.com

Publishing History
First Faery Rose Edition, 2009
Print ISBN 1-60154-519-3

Published in the United States of America

Dedication

To Alexia, who helped me believe
and
To Susan, who started it all

Author's Note

Hidden Cove was inspired by an actual location in the
Appalachians, and the inscription on the blackboard was
based on a real event.

Prologue

The only tree he could see was bare of leaves now, looking naked and cold in the slanting autumn light. He wondered if it would survive the winter. He knew he would not. He shifted in his chair and forced his focus away from the window and back into the room.

The newspaper reporter appeared out of nowhere and seated herself opposite him. She was young and perky, with a peculiar shade of red hair and fingernails to match. She had eager eyes and posture, and, he could tell, was painfully new at her job. He turned to look at her, and she smiled. Then she began to practice her skills at Putting the Subject at Ease.

She wanted to know all about his life—every detail. Since he had reached the century mark, it seemed everyone suddenly wanted to hear what he had to say. At age ninety-nine no one cared, but now...now everyone seemed to think he harbored some magical secret he might be persuaded to reveal. He sighed and pulled his thoughts back to the young woman. He tried his best to answer her questions, to describe how life was 'back then' as she put it. But it was difficult. It didn't seem so long ago to him, and it made him sad when he thought on some of it. But he didn't want to give her a sad story, especially since she was trying so hard, so he cleared his throat and told her about the fun and unusual things, like getting an indoor bathroom, or what it was like when electricity first came to the mountain.

Then she said: "Do you have any regrets about

anything in your life? Anything you would change if you could?"

The side of his mouth bent into a wry smile, and his gaze traveled out past the window again. He began to recede into another place. The reporter fidgeted, unsure how to pull him back. Abruptly he turned back toward her and said, "No. I've had a good life. An excellent, exciting—and different life. I have no regrets. I don't believe in regrets." He paused. Then, in a whisper, it slipped out. "I only wish I hadn't outlived my family."

She stopped writing and looked up from her pad, staring at him with a mixture of—what? Pity? Sadness? Then, suddenly, she disappeared, and he found himself staring out the window again, looking at nothing. He spent most of his time doing that exact thing lately. Staring at nothing. Waiting. Trying to find some bit of interest beyond the glass in the asphalt parking area. Trying to coax his focus away from the strange green fluorescent glow of his room. Desperately trying to concentrate enough to block out his immediate environment. His gaze moved to his watch for the hundredth, or perhaps millionth time, and his heart lurched. *This was it.* It was finally time. He knew where he had to go and what he had to do—what he urgently needed to do—despite his shaking hands. He had to go now. Immediately. Because they had planned it out together, in detail, many many years ago.

Chapter One

She noticed him as soon as they sat down. He sat alone at the counter, absorbed in his lunch, which included a ham sandwich and a large glass of milk. He looked out of place somehow, like he should be sporting a black tie, caressing a stemmed glass, and leaning suggestively against a mantel—not eating a meal in an old dime store.

Hadleigh nudged Jann under the table and jabbed her fork in his direction.

"What's wrong with that picture?" she demanded. "I can't put my finger on it."

Jann studied him as she opened her napkin.

"I don't know what you're talking about. He's cute." She giggled. "He looks a little like Elvis Presley."

Hadleigh looked at him out of the corner of her eye. He did look a little like Elvis, but not quite so baby-faced. His chin was chiseled, but not too extreme, and his cheekbones were high, but not overly pronounced. His body was well developed with a deep tan, his hands large and strong. *He looks like the kind of man you could put your confidence in.*

"He just seems so out of place somehow," she said finally.

"Well, I would consider Elvis being here *definitely* out of place." Jann's eyes twinkled. "I know what it is! It's the *milk*. REAL men don't drink milk," She winked.

Hadleigh laughed. "Not in public, you mean."

Jann returned her gaze to the counter, and then looked back at Hadleigh with what had come to be known as That Look.

Hadleigh faked a groan. "Oh no. I don't even want to hear this."

"I think you should send him a refill on his milk."

Hadleigh stifled a laugh, leaned across the table and stared under her eyebrows at Jann. "I don't recall asking you to be the Entertainment Director on the cruise ship of my life."

"You didn't. I volunteered. See a need and fill it..."

"Hmmmph!" Hadleigh straightened up and smiled. "In other words, I'm stuck with you and your creative meddling."

Jann nodded. "Absolutely."

"Why don't *you* send him a refill, since you're feeling all this motivation?"

"No, he's more your type. The milk and all."

Hadleigh kicked her under the table. "It would be fun, but I don't..."

"I dare you. Look, here comes the waitress. Come on, do something risky for a change. You might even like it."

"Good afternoon, ladies. Are you ready to order, or do you need a few minutes?"

"We're ready—we're just having dessert. I'll have the apple pie," Jann said with a daring glance at Hadleigh and a kick.

"I'll have the apple pie also...and...um...with ice cream on it...and umm..."

Another kick. Harder this time.

"Umm...could you please send the gentleman at the counter a refill on his milk?"

"Right away ladies." The waitress sauntered away without as much as a raised eyebrow.

Hadleigh buried her face in her hands. "Oh no—now I've done it! He could be an axe-murderer, or something."

Jann jaw dropped open in surprise. "I can't

believe you actually did it! Wow! My teaching has finally paid off!"

"Right. And you can feel guilty at my funeral, because it will be entirely your fault that I fell into the hands of a notorious serial killer."

"What an imagination! You should be a crime writer, not a dancer. Your talents are being entirely wasted."

Hadleigh laughed. "I suppose you're right. At least if he turns out to be a sordid character, and I somehow manage to escape his clutches, I can turn the experience into a best seller and retire to a tropical island." She sighed dramatically. "And all because of a glass of milk."

"And of course, you'll be taking your best friend—i.e. Entertainment Director—along. After all, the whole thing was my idea in the first place. That way I can continue tutoring you in the fine art of flirting. Which you will need desperately since your celebrity will cause untold hoards of men to follow you around. You'll also need my advice in weeding out all the weirdoes, and the ones just interested in being your arm candy. Although he certainly would make a pretty fine arm piece! Don't you think?"

Hadleigh glanced over at him again and noticed how the defined muscles in his back were evident even through his shirt. She looked away, suddenly embarrassed by the thoughts crossing her mind. She cleared her throat. "He certainly would."

"Speaking of candy and sweet things—here comes our apple pie. And ta da—look what else is on her tray—The Milk!"

Resisting the urge to cancel the whole thing, Hadleigh held her breath and closed her eyes. The waitress placed the plates in front of them, and then walked back behind the counter.

"Tell me what he does, Jann. I can't look. I feel like an idiot. Why do I let you talk me into these things?"

"Brace up, silly. He isn't even looking in our direction. Besides, you let me talk you into these *things*, as you so colorfully put it, because it's fun and exciting."

Hadleigh shrugged. It was true; Jann could make something as mundane as a visit to the dry cleaner an adventure. Hadleigh often wished she could be more like Jann. Fearless.

The waitress spoke a few words to the mystery man, and set the milk down in front of him. He nodded and continued eating.

"Well, I never!" Jann steamed. "What a jerk! He didn't even look in our direction! Not even a nod! He could have at least turned around! You'd think he expected strange women in restaurants to send him things. Humph! He's *worse* than an axe murderer!" Jann fumed.

Hadleigh let out her pent up breath. "I'm relieved. I should know better than to let you talk me into such absurdity. Let's just eat and forget him." She dug into her pie.

"Right. Nothing like apple pie to ease the pain of a broken heart."

Although stung by his rudeness, Hadleigh decided to ignore him and enjoy her splurge on dessert. She seldom allowed herself such indulgences, since keeping her 110-pound figure was essential if she intended to keep her job. The ballet company management was not sympathetic about weight gains in their dancers. But she and Jann had been blessed with the type of metabolism that could withstand a few splurges. She knew many dancers who were not as lucky.

Hadleigh had grown up with this type of self-discipline. She began ballet lessons at age eight and knew, even at that tender age, there was no other career for her. She loved every part of it. The precise exercises, the challenge of each new step, and the music—oh! She especially loved the music. She began her training with the usual one class per week, adding more classes each year until by age thirteen she practically lived at the dance academy run by her mother's sister, her beloved Aunt Pat. Pat was not only Hadleigh's dance teacher, but also her adopted mother, since she had raised Hadleigh almost from birth.

During her senior year in high school, Hadleigh began sending out résumés and auditioning for every company she could find. When graduation came and went and she still hadn't received any offers, she began to think she'd made a mistake. Perhaps she wasn't good enough to be a professional dancer after all. Then, in mid-summer, while she waited tables and took dance classes, two different companies called.

She selected Dance Imperial, a small but respected company based in Manhattan. When not performing in the city, they toured extensively, and were now on the home stretch of an eight-week journey up and down the eastern coast of the U.S. They were on the second of a three day residency in Orlando, then on to Miami, then home to New York. Hadleigh sighed. It would feel good to get home. She loved traveling and seeing new places, but she hated living out of a suitcase.

"Earth to Hadleigh," Jann whispered. "Don't look now, but the man of your dreams is leaving."

Hadleigh watched, trying to be discreet, as he finished off his second glass of milk, laid a tip on the counter, and walked up to the cash register. He spoke with the waitress while she rang up his amount, and then he vanished out the door, without so much as a backward glance.

"Well, we can tell everyone we observed one of the world's all-time-great-jerks at lunch today," sighed Hadleigh. She still thought him immensely attractive, although extraordinarily rude and strange.

"Cheer up! If we hurry, we'll have time for a nice, long nap before our call." Jann never missed an opportunity to nap, but perhaps that accounted for her energetic performances on stage.

The waitress appeared with their check, smiled at Hadleigh, and handed her a folded napkin.

"From the gentleman. He's an interesting character, sort of inside himself, and as usual, on a tight schedule. Just like all those doctors at the convention. Always rush, rush, rush. It's a wonder they don't die of indigestion."

"He's a doctor?" Jann jaw dropped. "Do you know him?"

"Not really. He's just been coming in here to eat, and the other day he forgot to remove the ID badge from his lapel, and well, I just happened to notice the name. Doctor Collins. Such a great name, you know—the kind you can put your confidence in. He mentioned staying at the hotel down the way. I don't wonder that you noticed him. He's a looker, alright. Kinda quiet, though, like I said. But if I were about twenty years younger..." She scooped up the plates and walked away, humming to herself.

"Come *on!*" Jann said, exasperated. "What does Dr. Prince Charming say?"

Hadleigh unfolded the napkin. "He appears to be a man of few words," she said, somewhat puzzled, "but at least he acknowledged us after all."

Jann grabbed the napkin. On it was one word. *Thanks.*

"Well, now you can relax," Jann said, wadding up the note and lobbing it back at Hadleigh. "Because he's definitely not an axe murderer. He's just plain obnoxious. Not even 'thank you.' Just 'thanks.' I guess he was just too pressed for time."

Hadleigh ducked as the napkin flew by her ear. She scraped up the last melted bit of ice cream from her plate and grabbed her dance bag, but not before she retrieved the wrinkled napkin and slipped it carefully into her bag.

"Come on, let's get back to the hotel. I've had enough adventure for one day. I'm ready to get back to a nice safe room and a nice safe theater."

During the walk back to the hotel, Hadleigh mused, half to herself, "I wonder what hotel the waitress was talking about. How many hotels are near here? Maybe he's staying in ours. Although I don't remember seeing anything about a convention."

"Can't get him out of your mind, huh? I can see the headlines now." Jann held out an imaginary newspaper: "Famous Dancer Slain by Almost-Psychotic Killer. Details at eleven."

"Aren't you confusing your mediums?" Hadleigh retorted. "I was just wondering if we would be bumping into Dr. Milk in the elevator or something."

"I think it's more like the 'or something.' How come you're so interested in romantic adventure all of a sudden?"

Hadleigh ignored her. They entered the hotel lobby. It looked like a thousand others, and reeked of that hotel-disinfectant smell. The room was empty, and there was nothing to indicate a large gathering of any kind, except for a small sign announcing a meeting of the Philately Association. The lone clerk had her back turned, watching a tiny television. There was obviously no medical convention here. It was too quiet.

"So sorry to disappoint you," Jann laughed, "but he must be at some other establishment. Maybe we could do some heavy spying later on! What do you say? It would be an unusual way of 'taking in the sights.' don't you think?!"

"I think you need a nap."

"Only moments ago you sounded suspiciously like you were ready for more risk taking. What happened? Speaking of which, how did you ever get into this dance business, anyway, with such a terminally underdeveloped sense of adventure? How can you make your living performing in front of thousands of people and be such a chicken?" She sighed. "I can see I'm destined to teach you how to *live!*" This was a familiar argument of Jann's.

"Well, you can teach me how to live later. Right now we have other obligations—like dancing in front of hundreds. Not thousands. *You* are having delusions of grandeur." Hadleigh rubbed her temples, a wave of fatigue washing over her. It was probably just the stress of being on the road for so many weeks. Any new person at all was interesting after living and traveling with the same people day in and day out. Although there was only one person in the company she truly disliked, too much togetherness can fray nerves to the breaking point.

But she had to admit it—she had found this man exciting. More than exciting. He was compelling, and that had never happened before. Why she found such a rude man so enticing she couldn't understand, especially since she had only observed him from a distance. It didn't make sense. Hadleigh seldom felt a need for anything outside her career and few close friends, and her few attempts at romance had been disasters. She long ago concluded that a dancer cannot hold any man's attention for long, and most of them disappear when they find out what a large time commitment dance requires. Hadleigh had never met any man that tempted her enough to give up—or even tone down—her career aspirations, and she never expected to.

"Honestly! You *are* a mess. You have to *push* the button to get the elevator, and you're just staring at it." Jann reached around her and jabbed the button hard.

"I'm sorry. I guess I must be feeling the stress of the tour, or something."

"Ah—once again—I think it's the 'or something.'

Come on, I think you're the one who needs a nap."
Jann nudged her into the elevator.

****

The performance that evening was a mixed
program, consisting of two classical pas de deux, one
solo piece, and two long balletic works
choreographed by their director, Adam Newsome.
Since neither Hadleigh nor Jann had yet achieved
the status of principal dancer, they were both cast as
corps de ballet members in the longer works.
However, one of the evening's pieces had a short
emotional solo in it for Hadleigh. She hoped this role
might mean that she was being considered for a
promotion to soloist, so she spent many long
rehearsal hours in the studio polishing it. She also
spent much of her personal time honing the acting
details. The bathtub or shower provided an
uninterrupted spot of time that served that purpose
well. Jann often commented that the only private
time a dancer had was while getting pruney in the
bathtub.

The solo was one of her favorite things to
perform because it was lyrical and dramatic. She
played the part of The Poet's Muse, and it suited her
perfectly. Her long hair cascaded down her back, and
an offstage fan blew toward her as she entered with
tiny bourreés that carried her across the mist-
shrouded stage. To the audience, she appeared to be
actually floating. The combination of the fan, the
lighting, and her invisible steps always drew a few
ahhhs from the audience. But tonight's performance
was witnessed by an audience member who would
have been impressed without the special effects. He
had come reluctantly, hesitant to get himself
involved in something he couldn't control. Yet he felt
compelled, for some odd overwhelming reason, and
so he purchased a ticket high in the balcony where
he thought—hoped—he could disappear.

At the end of the performance, as Hadleigh took

her solo bow, a "Bravo" rang out from high in the back of the theater. She heard it and thrilled to it, since that solo seldom elicited such an enthusiastic response.

Winded, Hadleigh paused in the wings to loosen the ribbons on her shoes.

"Who did you plant in the audience tonight? Is your *mother* visiting?" The barbed questions came from behind her. Hadleigh whirled around to confront Jasmine Shanell, one of the company's principal dancers, and the only member Hadleigh had little respect for.

"I don't know what you're talking about," Hadleigh replied, moving as fast as she could toward the dressing rooms. Jasmine just smirked and walked away, having fulfilled her modus operandi of undermining her competition.

Hadleigh entered her dressing room and closed the door a bit harder than necessary. But that lone "Bravo" put her in too good a mood to let Jasmine ruin it, despite the fact that she was an expert at mood destruction.

Jann looked up as the door slammed. "Don't tell me. Old Jas-gas is at it again, right?"

Hadleigh nodded. "There are days when I would love to slash her shoulder straps right before *Black Swan Pas de Deux.*"

"But you wouldn't. Have you considered itching powder in her tights? It's ever so much more subtle."

"I *refuse* to let her bother me tonight, but I'll save the idea for future reference."

The intercom crackled to life. "Hadleigh Brent, there's a parcel for you in the green room."

"I'll bet Jasmine left you a booby-trapped box of flowers! You better watch it!" Jann was only half kidding. "I mean it. You're getting too close to stepping on her toes. No pun intended. I better go down with you." She grinned.

"I don't know what I ever did to deserve you.

Imagine the risk you're taking. We could both be blown to bits. What a friend." Hadleigh feigned swooning against the dressing table.

"Well come *on*. The suspense is killing me." Jann dragged her out by the arm.

In the green room, Hadleigh found a small square box with her name on it. It was definitely suspicious looking.

"Hmmm. I'll bet it *is* from Jasmine. Something will probably jump out at you when you open it, so brace yourself," Jann warned, taking a step back.

Hadleigh held it gingerly at arm's length and inch by inch, eased it open. Nothing jumped. She peered in. It contained a small plastic bottle of milk and a note written in an authoritative, masculine hand. It read:

> *The enclosed is for a toast to your stunning*
> *performance this evening.*

There was no signature, only a phone number.

Hadleigh almost dropped the box. "I don't believe it!"

Jann grabbed the note. "Wow!" she said, dumbstruck. Then her wits returned. "Wait a minute. I bet this is still Jasmine's doing. She may have set you up for a bad practical joke."

"Hmmm. You might be right. Although I never gave her credit for having that much romantic creativity. I mean, we're talking about someone who chooses her lingerie according to what looks best on the floor." Hadleigh flashed a wicked grin at Jann, then sobered. "Noooo, something like this would take too much of her precious class and rehearsal time to prepare. It just doesn't sound like something she would do—and besides—how would she know about the milk this afternoon? It *must* be the man from the restaurant."

"Oh, how romantic! Dancer meets dashing

stranger during lunch, then they fall in love and live happily ever after. Go ahead! *Call him!*"

Hadleigh studied the note. Even if it was legitimate, she didn't think calling a stranger's hotel room was such a good idea. Always the conservative, she hesitated.

Never one to waste time, Jann pushed Hadleigh toward the pay phone. "There's no time *like* the present to thank the man *for* the present!"

"He hasn't even had time to get back to his hotel yet!" Hadleigh protested. "And besides, I don't want to look too anxious."

"I'm sure it's his cell phone number, so it doesn't matter, does it? Got any other excuses?" She stopped and stared at Hadleigh, hands on her hips. "Okay. I'll tell you what. We'll go back to the hotel, and that will give him time to get back to his room so he doesn't have to talk to you while he's out on the street somewhere. It will also give *me* time to bolster *your* courage."

"Okay." Hadleigh tried to summon up some of Jann's style of daring, but it didn't come easily to her. *How can I perform aggressively on stage and yet be so shy in private life?* She decided it must have something to do with the fact that stage performances are always well rehearsed, and life— well, life was just one long ad-lib. Onstage there was at least a modicum of control, and she had the comfort of always knowing the ending.

Upstairs in the dressing room, Jann removed her make-up in record time and began pacing the floor. Hadleigh procrastinated, wiping off her lipstick, blush, and make-up base with meticulous strokes.

"If you don't hurry up, he'll have moved six times and left forwarding addresses in three states."

Hadleigh threw a wadded up tissue in her direction. "I don't see why this is so important to you. You have no deficit of gentleman admirers, so why start in on me?"

"Because I feel responsible for finding a soul mate for my best friend, that's why." Jann stopped pacing and added, "And besides, I set you up for this whole thing in the first place, and I feel, well, sort of responsible."

"Well, first of all, I am not interested in husband-hunting. I am quite happy with my life the way it is. I have *never* had any great matrimonial aspirations. When I stop dancing, I plan to move to a remote but charming small town and open a small dance studio which will support me until I'm old and gray. So there." Hadleigh squinted, pulling off her false eyelashes. "And you think I should call him! A strange—a *very* strange, remember—man in a strange city in a strange hotel? You must be craaazy." Hadleigh started placing make-up brushes one at a time in her old tackle box.

"If you don't, you'll always wonder what might have been." Jann waved her arms exotically in front of Hadleigh's face. "And besides, I've never believed you and this old-maid scenario you've dreamed up. Nope, I don't buy it for a second! You're every bit— no I take that back—you're *more* romantic than most people I know. You just think that's some kind of big secret. But I know better." She pulled Hadleigh out of her chair. "Get a move on. I can't handle the suspense any longer."

Fifteen minutes later, they clicked open their hotel room door, and Jann rushed over to the phone, presenting it to Hadleigh with a flourish.

"Here you are, madam. Prince Charming awaits on the other end. And no, I will *not* dial the phone for you."

"Honestly, I don't know why I put up with you!" Hadleigh grabbed the receiver and replaced it. "I don't think I will call. It's just too risky." She plopped down on the bed, and glared at Jann. "Don't raise your eyebrows at me. If he wanted to see me, he could have come backstage. I think something's fishy somewhere."

Jann grabbed the note and began punching buttons on the phone. "Here!" She thrust the phone at Hadleigh. "It's ringing, so you better think fast!"

Hadleigh grabbed for it just as a deep voice answered with a smooth "Hello?"

"Hello, this is Hadleigh Brent." She couldn't quite keep the nervous tremor out of her voice.

"Yes? Who did you wish to speak to?"

"...ummm...ah...the gentleman who left the uh...package backstage."

"I am so sorry, but you must have the wrong number."

"Oh, I *am* sorry." Hadleigh dropped the receiver like it was a serpent and belly-flopped onto the bed with a loud "AAARGH!"

Jann stared at her. "Give me that phone; I must have punched in the wrong number. Sooo sorry. Will try again. This time I'll even get him on the line *for* you. Wimp."

Hadleigh threw a pillow in her direction.

Jann spoke in her best business tone. "Hello. Is Dr. Collins there please? Miss Hadleigh Brent calling."

Hadleigh covered her face.

Jann continued. "Oh. I am sorry for disturbing you again. Thank you. Good-bye."

She slammed the receiver down. "Okay, so you were right. Whoever the creep is, he gave you a fake number." She shrugged. "It takes all kinds. So much for a great romantic fling." She flopped back onto her bed. "At least you got a calcium-rich snack out of the deal."

Hadleigh gasped. "I'm not going to drink it! It could be laced with who-knows-what."

"So now he's a coward who resorts to poison, eh? And what would his motive be, pray tell? He's a sociopath who likes to kill young women who send him refills? Now there's an unbelievable plot line. Don't give up your day job." Jann stretched out on the bed, kicking off her shoes. "Well, I guess you shouldn't drink it, just to be safe. Come on, let's get some sleep. You know how cranky I am without enough sleep."

"That's for sure," Hadleigh said, studying the note again. "What number did you dial? This last number could be a seven or a one." *He certainly lives up to the stereotypical illegible doctor.*

"Hmmm." Jann squinted at the number. "I do believe you're right, Sherlock. It's a seven, not a one. Let's have another go at it!" She reached for the phone.

Hadleigh got up and intercepted her.

"My courage has returned. I'll take over from here." Taking a deep breath she punched the numbers.

"It's ringing."

"Amazing." Jann grinned.

"Still ringing." Hadleigh frowned. "I guess he must have gone...Hello? This is Hadleigh Brent calling." Her hands began shaking, and she sat down hard on the bed.

"Miss Brent! How wonderful! I thoroughly enjoyed your performance this evening. It was the highlight of my week," he said, his tone of voice deep and sincere. "Thank you for calling. I wasn't sure you would. I'm afraid my behavior at the restaurant today was inexcusable, so I won't offer any excuses."

"None required. Thank you for the compliment. Oh, and the milk!"

"There is a little something else I didn't include with your gift," he said, "but I have it here if you think you might be interested."

Hadleigh hesitated. "Really? What is it?"

"Two straws."

Hadleigh laughed, and began to relax. "How interesting."

"Would you like them delivered? I could arrange it."

"Well...I...uh..."

"Of course! I forgot how late it's getting to be, and I'm sure you must be tired after your performance. How about breakfast tomorrow? At that charming little place where we both know the waitress?"

"I'd like that."

"Eight o'clock too early?"

"No, perfect."

Chapter Two

Hadleigh jumped out of bed at dawn, and began pacing up and down, throwing one rejected outfit after another into a pile. Jann finally heaved a pillow at her.

"Come on—*relax*. He's not publishing the year's best dressed list."

"Right." Hadleigh heaved the pillow back and wriggled into yet another outfit.

"And it's *breakfast*, remember. Not dinner with the Czar."

"I can always depend on you to keep a realistic outlook." She twisted back and forth, studying her reflection in the mirror. "Okay. How do I look?"

"Stunning. You'll be the hit of the breakfast rush. Now get out of here so I can catch a few extra winks." She grinned. "Good luck!"

"Thanks!"

Hadleigh stepped into the hall and tried to compose herself. Why she should be so nervous about a simple breakfast date disturbed her. Her emotions were usually as well trained as her body.

****

Hadleigh pushed the door open and glanced around the restaurant. She felt a flush as she saw him beckoning to her from a corner booth. He had papers spread out all over the table but swept them away when she approached.

"Good morning. I hope you slept well last night—hotels can sometimes be unsettling." He smiled and extended his hand.

"I slept well, thank you—I guess I'm almost getting used to hotel life." She felt his hand close

19

around hers—a warm, secure handshake that made her blush. She realized uncomfortably that she was having difficulty catching her breath. It wasn't *that* long a walk from the hotel.

She slid into the booth, and he settled himself across from her then offered his hand again.

"I guess I should introduce myself. Doctor Collins, at your service."

"Pleased to meet you." Hadleigh again felt the warm, strong grip of his hand and found herself trembling. She pulled her hand away, afraid he could feel it.

He cleared his throat. "So, tell me about yourself, Miss Brent."

"Please—call me Hadleigh."

"Okay. Hadleigh." He pronounced her name deliberately, as though savoring the syllables. "You can call me Doc. All my friends do."

"Okay, Doc."

"So, tell me, how did you come to have such an unusual profession?"

"Unusual? I guess I never thought it was particularly unusual, maybe because I grew up in it. I loved ballet and was lucky enough to be good at it, so there never seemed to be any other choice. It was all I ever wanted to do. I love everything—well, almost everything about it. The traveling to new places, the performing, even the classes and the rehearsals. Some dancers hate the repetition of class and the stress of rehearsals, but I never felt that way. Every day seems exciting to me because ballet is so challenging. You never really get it right—or at least as right as you want it to be. So you never get bored. Of course it's also beautiful to watch. I even enjoy watching the other dancers because, well— ballet is just *beautiful*." Hadleigh blushed. "I know that sounds pretty lame."

He watched her, studying her expressions as she spoke. Talking about her career caused her to become enthusiastic and animated. Her love for it was obvious and he could see she was more than a little devoted to it.

Hadleigh shifted, feeling uncomfortable under his scrutiny. "Wait a minute! I'm doing all the talking! I'm sorry. I get carried away when I talk shop. So what about you? What are your passions in life? Besides medicine, I mean." She cocked her head and gazed into those large blue eyes, so striking against his dark hair and tanned skin.

His eyes narrowed, and he looked at her for a long moment before he answered. "Well, I love the outdoors. Hiking, camping, and such. I like taking long walks through the woods after a rain and smelling the dampness. It makes me feel wonderful. I have a small place in the mountains that takes me out of the rush of the ordinary."

"I used to go camping when I was a child. I love the woods, too. Do you get to go there often?" she asked.

He hesitated. "Well, actually, I *live* there most of the time."

"You *live* there? I would have guessed you spend most of your down time lying on a beach—you have such a beautiful tan."

His face clouded. "No, I've never been a beach person, although I have spent a bit of time near the ocean. My real loves are the woods and mountains. My passions haven't changed since childhood." He smiled. "Like you."

****

Later, when Jann asked for "details." Hadleigh couldn't remember what they had talked about, only that they had talked so long that she almost missed her 10:00 class. If Jann hadn't come racing in, she would have, and dancers do not miss their 10:00 class. To do so once would arouse suspicion; twice would be artistic suicide. Class is considered sacred. Its repetition allows dancers to retain their physical conditioning and helps to hone their instrument. Class, to a dancer, is more than a job requirement. It can be a meditation, a comfort, or a trial. And for some, an obsession.

But today's class passed in a haze for Hadleigh. She hardly noticed when, rocking a bit as she balanced in retiré, she heard Jasmine hiss behind her, "Oh pleeeaasee. How am I supposed to balance with you doing that in front of me?"

The company schedule included two more performances—a matinee and an evening. It would be a long day, but Hadleigh hadn't hesitated when Doc asked her to join him for a late dinner after the show. For the first time she could remember, her mind wasn't on her work. She tried not to think about the fact that tomorrow the company would leave for Miami and she would never see him again. She tried to think like Scarlett O'Hara: "*I'll worry about that tomorrow.*"

The matinee was a different program, geared toward a younger audience, and it included the ballet *Peter and the Wolf*. Hadleigh danced the part of the Bird, and Jann the Duck. The costumes were elaborate and fun, and the choreography was a nice respite from some of the more technically demanding works from the classical repertoire, like *Swan Lake*. It was also a shorter performance, thus giving Jann a chance for one of her beloved power naps between shows.

****

He was mesmerized by her. Obscured by the shadows in the highest row of the theater, Doc watched Hadleigh perform in a simple children's ballet. Hidden under layers of feathers, she was almost unrecognizable, yet he was unable to take his eyes off her. He had come again to sit in the balcony, as if by watching from afar he could uncover the secret of this attraction. Once revealed, he could overcome it and go on about his business, and his life would remain uncomplicated. He hated having his life complicated. He'd had enough of that growing up, but managed to rid himself of that baggage (or so he hoped), and had gone on to establish a rewarding, although sometimes lonely, life for himself. Now this. This beautiful, shy lady had appeared and magically taken over his life, just like she did when she stepped on stage. He couldn't ignore her any more than he could have turned and walked out on her performance. Nor did he want to. But he knew he was opening the door to things better left alone.

****

When Hadleigh arrived at the theater that evening, she found a large bouquet of roses on her dressing table and an even larger amount of discussion and speculation going on around her. *Life in a dance company is anything but private, and gossip is the grease that fuels the cloistered society.*

"So Hadleigh—what sort of secrets have you been keeping from us?" said Lisa, one of the company's soloists. "Is this a new man in your life, or someone we just never heard about? Come on—'fess up!"

Hadleigh laughed. *Life in a goldfish bowl.* No information was sacred. "I just met him, and it's nothing, really," she said, pulling out the card.

"Those are some awfully fragrant nothings on your dressing table. What's his name? How did you meet him?"

"It was terribly mundane. I met him at a restaurant." She opened the card.

"So...what does the card say?" Lisa paused with one false eyelash in her hand and tried to read over Hadleigh's shoulder. "Is it romantic? Come on, share!"

Lisa was the company busybody, but she was so much fun that no one seemed to mind. She liked everyone, or gave a good impression of it, and everyone liked her. She had a knack for storytelling and could make getting her washer fixed sound like the most entertaining thing in the world.

"He just says *'Looking forward to tonight, Doc.'*"

The shrieks that ensued were deafening. "Ooooh...and what are the plans for tonight?" Lisa demanded.

Hadleigh sent her a mock glare. "Nothing like *that*. Take that R rating off your mind! We're just having dinner together after the performance. Okay?"

"Yeah, right. Jann, is that the real scoop—or is she holding out on us?"

"That's the real scoop. No lie."

"Hmmmph. Well, you know we'll all need *details* tomorrow."

Hadleigh just sighed and summoned up a tired smile.

This day had already dragged on so long that she thought it would never end. Usually these days, so crammed full of class, rehearsal, and performance, just flew by, one day blending into the next. Especially on tour, when one town or city became indistinguishable from the next, each day passed like all others, and the fatigue at the end of the day assured a solid, rock-like sleep. But now the world had changed—overnight. It seemed to have only two settings—slow motion or fast forward. Today was definitely the former. And sleep—well, last night she hardly slept at all, and surprisingly it hadn't seemed to bother her much today. Her mind was riveted on just one thing. She wanted time to speed up so she could get to the end of the day. It became a mantra that played over and over in her head: hurry up...hurry up...get to the end...get to the end.

"Hey! Come on, Miss Daydreamer! Time for warm-up." Jann learned over and whispered, "Try to keep your wits about you. Remember, we leave in the morning."

Hadleigh came back to reality with a start. *Leave in the morning! That's right. I can't let this man overwhelm me——he probably does this to lots of girls whenever he's at a medical convention. I'm letting my imagination run away with me.* Straightening her shoulders and resolving to concentrate on her performance, Hadleigh headed down onto the stage for warm-up.

Well. There was Jasmine—in Hadleigh's spot. Every dancer has an unspoken, or sometimes a very spoken, "spot" at the barre. There is a code of honor among dancers—you don't take someone's spot. If this is done, it indicates an attempt to intimidate or irritate. Or gossip. Jasmine was undoubtedly trying to do all three.

Hadleigh, feeling uncharacteristically aggressive and in no mood to be manipulated, stormed over and stood in front of her, just inches away, like Jasmine was invisible. Everyone on the stage became quiet.

"Pleeeease. Must we insist on our petty little spots? I think it's time some of us grew up around here. Look, there's plenty of room on the other side." Jasmine swept her hand across the barre to indicate where, as though Hadleigh were a clueless child.

Hadleigh stared at her, her face flushing. "Really? You mean I can have *your* spot? I am sooo not worthy." She walked around the barre and began stretching.

A door slammed and the sound of rapid footsteps heralded the arrival of Tom, the ballet master. The dancers immediately reverted to their normal routine. Jasmine turned her back and went on with her own warm-up like nothing had happened.

"Okay people, one more time. Just take it easy and get those muscles going. We'll do the usual pliés." Tom nodded toward the pianist. "Four please."

Still steamed, Hadleigh tried to let the music soothe her. She hated having her temper get the best of her. She knew it just fueled Jasmine's fire, and she felt embarrassed that she had lost control in front of everyone. Thank goodness Tom was running a little late today. She didn't want the management thinking they had a dancer who wasn't a team player. Jasmine's status meant she was too valuable to ever get into any real trouble. She sold too many tickets, not to mention the fact that she just happened to be married to the company director. Definitely a no-win situation.

Warm-up concluded without any further complications, and everyone returned to their dressing rooms. Fortunately, Jasmine's principal status allowed her a room all to herself. This pleased her and everyone else.

"Hey! What's gotten into you? You sure told Jas-gas what for!" Jann's eyes widened in amazement.

"Boy it's great to see someone stand up to her once in a while!" Lisa logged in, laughing. "But you're the last person I expected to do it!"

The support made her feel better, but Hadleigh never enjoyed making a scene.

"Well, I wish I hadn't done it." Hadleigh said. "Now I'll keep waiting for the other shoe to drop." She tried to laugh.

"Don't you mean the other pointe shoe?" Jann tried to add some humor—to no avail.

"And that it will. She's not going to let you get off without something," Lisa added dryly. "You better watch your back."

Hadleigh sighed. Lisa was right. Now the subtle rivalry that had simmered between them since Hadleigh achieved that soloist role seemed to be maturing into an outright war. Jasmine had never let anyone progress into even equal status, much less threaten her position. It was now apparent. She must feel very threatened.

****

After the performance, Doc found his way

backstage. Upstairs, Hadleigh heard the sound she had longed for all day—the intercom announcing, "Miss Brent, you have a visitor in the green room."

She showered and removed her make-up in record time. Then she slipped into the one evening-style outfit she carried with her on every tour. It was a simple little black dress—but one she knew looked elegant on her. Hadleigh always packed it for the inevitable receptions that happened following opening nights in each city. These affairs were a part of her job she didn't mind, since it was about the only time she got to hear any positive comments on her performances. Some of her fellow dancers preferred to slip out early to party on their own—it gave them a chance to mingle with people not associated with the company.

In the green room, Doc managed to locate a small chair. It was a poor fit for his six-foot-two frame, but he compressed himself into it and waited. This environment was strange to him, yet he found it fascinating. *These dancers look so different offstage.* Most were much tinier than they appeared on stage, many only an inch or two over five feet tall. Then there was the make-up—it looked so wild—large, exaggerated eyes and lips of brilliant red. He tried to picture Hadleigh like that but couldn't. He had grown up with the idea that lots of make-up on a woman was unnecessary; perhaps even an indication of a loose woman. He knew that wasn't true, but the teachings of childhood die hard.

Jasmine wandered through and stopped across the room from Doc. She appeared to be engrossed in the information posted by the old pay phone. Doc noticed her and remembered her performance. Judging from the audience's reaction he knew she must be talented, but he hadn't enjoyed her dancing at all. He found it uninspiring, although apparently technically solid, and it made him wonder how one's ability was judged in this strange new world.

Jasmine lingered a long time before returning to her dressing room. It was within earshot of the green room, and she left the door cracked.

Soon Hadleigh appeared, and Doc rose to greet her.

"Once again, a stunning evening. I was impressed."

Hadleigh flushed. "Thank you. You weren't bored seeing the same pieces again?"

"On the contrary. I noticed little details this time that I had missed before."

"Uh-oh. Maybe it would be better if you only came once. I don't want you to start seeing all the flaws!"

The crack in Jasmine's door widened.

"Shall we? I reserved a table at a place I think you will enjoy. It has a beautiful view of the city, and the food is wonderful. Although I'm afraid it doesn't have the waitress we both know." He smiled. "Do you think we can handle that?"

Hadleigh laughed. He made her feel so many things all at once—happy, nervous, hopeful, and for lack of a better word—special.

"I think I can tough it out. Change is good."

He eased the dance bag off her shoulder, and slipped his arm across her back to lead her out. She felt the penetrating warmth of his hand and leaned toward him as they moved past Jasmine's door. He smelled so good, but Hadleigh couldn't decide if he was wearing any cologne.

They walked the few short blocks to the restaurant, located at the top of a large high-rise. Already packed with the after-theater crowd, it was obviously the local place to see and be seen. Doc spoke to the maitre'd, and he nodded and escorted them to a small, dark booth in the far back corner of the restaurant, overlooking the city lights.

"Is this okay for you?" Doc asked. "I thought you might like to be out of the spotlight for a while."

"It's perfect."

Hadleigh slid in and he settled himself beside her. She could feel the comforting warmth of his body and with each breath she took, she inhaled his delicious scent. She still couldn't decide if he was wearing cologne.

The waiter appeared and inquired about their wine selection. Hadleigh seldom drank wine, and knew little about it, so Doc ordered for them both. She hated being so un-worldly, but it came with the territory of the cloistered dancer life. Most of her colleagues seemed to be at one end of the spectrum or another. Either they were anti-alcohol, or they rebelled and smoked and drank to excess. She noticed that those in the latter category seldom had a long career.

When the wine arrived, Doc raised his glass. "What shall we toast to? Any suggestions?"

Hadleigh pursed her lips. "Hmmm. Dare I say to chance encounters?"

"At luncheon counters." He laughed. "Excellent! Here's to chance encounters." He paused, his expression clouding. He looked at her for a long moment, then said softly, "May ours prove to be but an inkling of things to come."

Hadleigh felt a shiver go through her. They raised their glasses and gently clinked them together. Hadleigh looked into his eyes. *Those stunning eyes! People must often comment on his eyes*. They were now focused on her with an intensity that made her both happy and afraid. Happy just to be here beside him, and afraid she might not ever feel this way again. But the delicious warmth of the wine soon washed away Hadleigh's fears, at least for the moment.

He slid closer and put his arm around her. He picked up a menu. "What is your most favorite food in the world? If you could have anything you wanted?"

Hadleigh smiled. "That's easy. Ice cream. I have always been a pushover for ice cream. So many flavors, so little time!"

He smiled. "Now, I would have expected you to say chocolate. Or perhaps something exotic, like Oysters Rockefeller or—I don't know—baked Alaska, maybe."

"Why? Because I'm a ballet dancer, you think my tastes must be exotic?" She cocked her head, puzzled.

"Well, no—it's because I thought most women preferred chocolate over anything."

Hadleigh pounced on the opportunity. "Chocolate *is* good over anything." Then she added mischievously, maybe because of the wine, "and I am *not* most any woman."

He reached over with his free arm and brushed a stray lock of hair back off her face. "Of that I am well aware," he whispered.

They did dine exotically—at least in Hadleigh's mind. They began with appetizers of oysters on the half shell and progressed to an entree of roast chicken with all the trimmings. Later, when the waiter returned to inquire whether or not they would care for dessert, Doc said, "Yes. We would like to share a large ice cream sundae with your best hot fudge sauce."

Hadleigh interrupted, "But please leave off any nuts."

"Very good, ma'am."

Doc smiled at Hadleigh. "I hope that wasn't too presumptuous of me, but I thought we might be able to choke it down."

"I think so."

As the waiter cleared the plates, Doc again placed his toned arm around her shoulders. She nestled close to him, despite having reservations about allowing herself to move this fast. But she found it irresistible, this feeling of being protected and admired, and she couldn't help herself.

The dessert arrived in a large ice-cream-parlor dish and smothered in chocolate. It looked delicious. Hadleigh reached for her spoon, but he brushed her hand away.

"Allow me," he said.

He dipped in his spoon and fed her the first bite. It was cold and sensuous and good. The best she had ever tasted. She licked a tiny bit of chocolate off her lips.

"Now it's my turn," she said, filling up the spoon, being sure to get equal amounts of ice cream and chocolate. She raised it to his lips and they closed over it. He took it in slowly...slowly...savoring the flavor and the feeling.

A bit of chocolate ended on his chin, and she brushed it off with her finger.

He reached for her hand and placed her finger to his lips, gently kissing the chocolate off. Hadleigh's whole body trembled. He moved on and kissed each finger in turn until she became so light-headed she feared she might faint. He traced her cheek with two fingers, and she turned her face toward his caress. His fingers brushed her lips. They lingered there for a moment then ran underneath her chin, lifting her face to him. Her eyes closed. Just when she thought she couldn't stand it anymore, he kissed her. His touch was gentle at first, just a brush of his warm lips against hers. Then he pressed harder, deeper, holding her closer, until she could no longer catch her breath.

Overwhelmed by the sensations coursing through her, Hadleigh forced herself to push him away. Embarrassed and remembering where she was, she looked guiltily around the restaurant. She needn't have worried. The room had emptied of everyone except one couple on the far side of the room.

Doc cupped her face in his hands. He looked long

into her eyes and caressed her cheek again with two strong fingers, as though trying to memorize its contours.

"What are we going to do, Miss Brent? What are we going to do?" His voice, tinged with a strange, wistful sadness, made Hadleigh's heart ache. Abruptly Doc put his hands back down on the table and straightened up. "I think it's time to see you home," he said, his demeanor all business again.

He motioned to the waiter, while Hadleigh stared out the window. What *were* they going to do? She had to leave with the company tomorrow. Would she ever see him again? If she did, would it be the same? Or was this just a magic night—a momentary fling, never to come again, brought on by the unfamiliar surroundings and a longing for something or someone to make it special?

He walked her back to the hotel in silence. Hadleigh said nothing, afraid any words might break the spell. *I feel like Cinderella.* At the same time, she recognized the absurdity of the idea. One wonderful fantasy night, and then poof! The clock strikes twelve and it's all over. *I hardly think he'll mount his trusty steed and travel the world to find me.* And she realized she hadn't a clue about where to find him. In fact, she knew almost nothing about him. He had skillfully allowed her to do most of the talking.

Stopping in the hotel lobby, Doc broke the silence. "May I call you again? If so, *where* might I find you?" He paused, running his hand through his hair. "This is getting complicated, isn't it?"

Hadleigh nodded. She rustled through her purse and found the company itinerary. She copied down the phone number and name of the Miami hotel.

"I don't know what room I'll be in, but just ask for me. Then we can talk about how we can do this." She hesitated, then said in a low voice, "I do want to see you again."

He gathered her into his arms, and she allowed her body to melt against him. He kissed her again, longer, deeper, richer than before. A kiss to last a long time—a kiss to be remembered.

****

Hadleigh stared out the window of the bus and watched the endless countryside roll by. Not much to see, just woods on each side and the eternity of yellow highway lines skipping by in the middle. She used to love travel days. It gave her time to rest her sore feet and an opportunity to see new things. But today every mile that ticked by just took her further and further from where she wanted to be.

Jann hadn't grilled her like she'd expected last night, maybe because of the late hour. Or maybe she was just amazed at how late it was. Hadleigh seldom stayed out later than midnight, especially at the end of a tour when energy levels were waning.

Soon Tom began making his usual rounds down the aisle. As rehearsal director, it fell to him to give the dancers notes on their performances and to let them know about any scheduling or casting changes. He came and sat down next to Hadleigh. This was not unusual. Every dancer expected to get constructive criticism on their performances in an effort to continually improve the quality of the company.

He forced a smile at Hadleigh. "There's been a small change in the program for tomorrow night." He cleared his throat. "Alison is going to be doing the *Poet's Muse* for a while." He shifted position, drumming his fingers on the armrest. "I don't have any other notes for you, except to end your variation in *Peter* a little more to stage right."

He got up without another word and moved on toward the rear of the bus, leaving Hadleigh reeling. Alison was Hadleigh's understudy. An apprentice just out of high school, this was her first tour with the company. Despite an obvious talent, she hadn't yet honed the artistry necessary for such a role. Or so Hadleigh thought. In fact, rumor had it that Alison wasn't even planning to stay with the company after her apprenticeship ended. She had her sights set on bigger companies in Europe.

Dumbfounded and hurt, Hadleigh blinked back tears. *Was there something wrong with her performance? Why hadn't Tom let her know?* He knew how hard she worked, and how willing she was to change anything that didn't seem right. *How could this be?*

Jann turned around and whispered over the seat. "You know this is Jasmine's doing. You didn't think she'd let you get away with confronting her like you did, did you? Pure nastiness—that's all it is. She whined to Adam about it, and he caved. Don't worry about it. This will all blow over, and you'll be dancing *Muse* again before you know it."

Hadleigh managed a weak smile. Jann was such a good friend, and she was undoubtedly right about Jasmine. But she wasn't so sure this wasn't a permanent demotion. Jasmine had never liked her and now must feel pretty threatened by her. Hadleigh knew all too well that Jasmine always got what she wanted. No one was indispensable in a dance company. No talent was great enough to provide rock-solid job security, and Hadleigh knew it.

She looked out the window and saw large black storm clouds gathering. *Perfect. That's just how I feel.* She hoped it would rain, and rain hard.

Rain hard it did. All day long. It slowed them down and made a normal six-hour drive stretch into eight. So they arrived late, tired and cranky—and the hotel was a rude surprise. It was old, deteriorating and located in a debatable-looking section of town. Someone hadn't done their homework. Although the company didn't provide five-star accommodations for their dancers, they did manage to house them in clean, moderately upscale establishments.

Regardless, they checked in, and Hadleigh and Jann went up the rebellious, clanking elevator to their room.

"Maybe we should have taken the stairs," Hadleigh complained.

"Ten flights?! I don't think so. I'm too tired now to even consider a single flight."

It seemed to take forever, but they managed to arrive at their floor without incident. No sooner had they thrown down their luggage and collapsed on the beds, than someone pounded on their door. Jann, instantly power-napping, bolted awake.

"Who is it?"

"It's Tom."

Hadleigh opened the door to confront a frazzled-looking Tom.

"I hope you didn't unpack. We're leaving for another place. This hotel can't provide secure parking for our equipment truck, and you know how Adam feels about that. He wants everybody downstairs in ten minutes."

"Okay."

Jann rolled over and groaned. "Well, at least I hadn't jumped in the shower yet."

"Come on. Maybe this time we'll get one with a better elevator."

"Yeah, and a room without the peeling wallpaper." Jann poked at a dangling strip. Hadleigh shuddered. She welcomed the change in accommodations, even though she was bone tired and it was past ten o'clock at night. This place gave her the creeps. It was only when they had finally unpacked at their new space that it hit her. Did the company leave information at the peeling hotel about where they were moving? Would Doc be able to find her if he called? Oh *why* hadn't she thought to get his address? Or at least his cell phone number? What an idiot. He hadn't offered it to her, and she had been so overwhelmed she hadn't thought to ask. It was way too late to ring Tom's room to see if he had given a forwarding address, and he had looked so worn out.

"What's the matter?" Jann demanded. "Other than everything I already know about?"

"Doc won't be able to call me now."

"So, call him."

Hadleigh didn't say anything, but her expression gave her away.

"Don't tell me. You never got his phone number?! Boy, you are one sick puppy!" She bounced down on the bed. "Don't worry. Of course the company left word where they can be reached. They can't afford not to. There are too many people that would need to know. So don't sweat it."

"Of course you're right—but I won't rest easy until he calls, anyway."

"Suit yourself." Jann lay back and closed her eyes, too tired for any more discussion. In a few minutes she was sound asleep. Hadleigh clicked off the lamp and slipped under the covers, but sleep didn't come. Wide awake, she stared up at the little red light on the smoke detector and prayed for the phone to ring, long after she knew it was far too late for him to call. She rolled back and forth for a long time, unable to find a comfortable position. It was near dawn before exhaustion overtook her and she finally dozed.

Chapter Three

Hadleigh awoke to Jann shaking her. "Come *on*, sleepyhead. It's a whole new day and there aren't any monumental blunders in it yet."

"Oh yes there are. The ones left over from yesterday. A big fat one named Jasmine."

"Forget her. She is nothing. Just keeping saying it. She is nothing. She is nothing. See? I feel better already!"

"Hmmph!" Hadleigh snorted. But she knew Jann was trying to cheer her up, so she tried to play along.

"She is nothing. She is nothing," she said, lurching around and trying to sound like low-voltage robot.

Jann howled. "Don't give up your day job."

"I hope I don't have to."

"Don't even go there. I won't let you. This is just a temporary set-back. Now, come *on* or we'll be late."

****

Hadleigh lay on the stage, stretching. She stared at the many colors in the lights over her head. They were off, but the brilliant colors of the gels were still striking. Every little girl dreams of being a ballerina, but no one ever tells them what that really means. Long days, low pay, dusty theaters, cookie-cutter hotels, and sore feet. *Really* sore, torn-up feet. *What a glamorous life.* Hadleigh felt so blue she forgot all about the things she loved. The excitement of a performance well done and well appreciated. Signing autographs, wearing fairy-tale costumes, seeing lots of different places. The thrill of hearing a "Bravo" from the balcony.

She tried not to think about him, but just picturing him in her mind felt so wonderful, it forced out every other thought. Then uncertainly followed, and it hurt too much.

Alison arrived and tiptoed to the other side of the stage. Although excited about getting Hadleigh's part, she still felt uncomfortable. She hadn't been associated with the company long enough to know exactly what was going on, but she was astute enough to realize that *something* was.

Hadleigh sighed, continued stretching, and tried to ignore the obvious effort from Alison to become invisible. She had nothing against Alison at all. In fact, she rather liked her. But it's harder to like someone when they've suddenly become more competition than bargained for. She knew this whole thing wasn't Alison's fault, she was just caught in the middle. Not that that made it any easier. Hadleigh's mood continued to self-destruct, and she began to wonder if her five years with the company had been a waste of time. She had joined thinking there was a good chance of promotion, especially since the company was small, but now she wasn't sure. The top ranks seemed to be sealed shut. But then, she second-guessed herself. *Am I dancing only because I want to be a "star" or because I love dancing? Is it because I like the power that comes from being admired?* She liked to think she danced because it gave her the opportunity to make people happy, but maybe that was just a way of rationalizing and making her pursuit seem unselfish. Staring at the unlit gels wasn't providing any answers, so she stood up and began doing relevés facing the barre—and facing away from Alison. Wonderful relevés! Great for strengthening one's feet, but also indispensable for working out frustration.

****

The evening's performance passed in a haze.

Hadleigh stayed in the dressing room during *Poet's Muse* but wasn't able to silence the backstage monitor, so she was forced to listen to the music. Jann tried to distract her by talking a blue streak, but it didn't help much. Hadleigh tried sewing ribbons on her pointe shoes to get a few pairs ahead, but she kept pricking her finger and the thread kept knotting up, so she gave up and tossed the whole mess in her dance bag. Then she just sat, legs propped up on the dressing table, taking long swallows from her water bottle in between staring at the concrete walls. It was just going to be one of those dark days to tough out, as her teachers used to say.

But, like all bad things, it finally came to an end. The performance ended at last. Worn out and sore, Hadleigh and Jann retired to their hotel room, instead of celebrating the end of the tour with the rest of the company.

"Did we get any messages?" Hadleigh said, as Jann walked by the phone.

"Afraid not. You could go check at the desk, just to be sure."

"I think I might just do that. Back in a flash." Hadleigh sprinted into the lobby and was just about to ask the desk clerk when Tom walked up behind her.

"Look," he said, looking around and lowering his voice, "I don't want you to get too upset about this. Alison did not perform well tonight. I think you'll be back doing *Muse* after the lay-off. Just remember— you didn't hear it from me." He walked away toward the elevators. Hadleigh dashed after him.

"Tom! Thank you. I really needed to hear that. Oh, wait. I have a question. Did you leave a forwarding address at the other hotel?"

"Of course. Why? Someone special you're expecting to hear from?" His eyes twinkled. "Yes, I *have* heard some rumors. You know there's nothing private in this dance company!"

Hadleigh blushed. "Well, I was sort of expecting a call, but it's no big deal."

Tom started back toward the elevators, then turned and said with a sly wink, "No big deal, huh? Somehow I just don't believe that!" Then he continued on without another word.

There was no message at the desk, so Hadleigh returned upstairs to bed, vowing to put Doc out of her mind. Completely. Forever. Erased for eternity. *Deleted.* She didn't need the complications of having a man in her life. She was quite happy with her career—well, maybe not at the moment, but most of the time. Or so she tried to convince herself before falling into an exhausted sleep.

****

On the bus the next morning, everyone was in good spirits, looking forward to going home and the two week lay-off period they had scheduled before returning to start the spring season. Jasmine was irritatingly perky and leaned over the seat to grill Hadleigh about the new man in her life.

"So. I hear you met someone. Is he cute? What does he do? Can he support you in the manner to which you have been accustomed?" She laughed, but her eyes narrowed.

Sure, Hadleigh thought. *She'd love to have me get married and leave the company. All the more for her.*

Jann chimed in. "Yes he *is* cute, and not only that, he's a doctor. So I guess support won't be problem."

Jasmine grimaced at Jann. "I wasn't speaking to you. I wanted to hear it from the horse's mouth. Ooops, sorry. Poor choice of words."

Jann just rolled her eyes.

"So, do you have some great rendezvous planned with him for this coming week? Flying to Tahiti or something?" Jasmine was relentless.

Hadleigh turned her face away.

"What's the matter? No rendezvous? Don't tell me. He said he'd call you." She snorted. "That's right up there with 'the check is in the mail.' or 'no, you don't look fat.' Pleeeaasee."

"Jasmine, hadn't you better get back to sewing your pointe shoes or something?" Jann said in a desperate attempt to silence her.

"Why? I want to know the scoop." She leaned closer to Hadleigh, and assumed the *I Know More about Life than You* attitude. "Well...you *do* know there are lots of men out there that are sort of, well, ballerina groupies. At least that's what I call them. It happened to me *a lot* before I married Adam. They follow you around, tell you how beautiful you are, send you flowers, take you to the most expensive places...et cetera, et cetera. But they don't *really* care about you. They're in love with the Ballerina Image. They'll do the same thing next week to another dancer, or actress, or whatever, in the next production that comes along." She sighed dramatically. "Sad, but true. I'm *so* glad I'm not out there anymore."

Hadleigh tried to tune her out.

"But then," Jasmine chirped, "Maybe that won't happen to you. Maybe you'll turn out to be one of the rare lucky ones. I have *heard* it can happen, even if the odds are sooo against it." Satisfied, she sat back down and returned to cross-stitching her ribbons.

Jann leaned in close to Hadleigh to perform damage control.

"Don't let her get to you," she whispered. "It's just what she wants. Besides, do you want to take advice from someone who picked her stage name from selections at a perfume counter?"

"I know, but the horrible thing is, she may be right."

"Well, you don't know that, so just let it go for now."

"I know you're right, of course, but I just don't feel like I'm bursting with optimism at the moment." Hadleigh sighed and turned away to stare out the window.

Jann went back to sewing her own shoes, not to be outdone by Jasmine. She did worry that Jasmine might be on to something. There *were* men who liked nothing more than having a series of dancers on their arm. Pretty arm pieces. They wined them and dined them and then went on to the next one. Some dancers loved it and didn't care to get any more involved, anyway, but Jann knew that Hadleigh wasn't one of them. Fiercely independent, she either wanted a man who would sweep her off her feet so they would live happily ever after, or she'd rather be alone. Up until now, Jann had always noticed—and rather admired—that Hadleigh never seemed to mind being alone. In fact, she seemed to thrive on it.

As if tuning in to the same wavelength, Hadleigh thought about how being alone with no significant other in her life had never bothered her. Until now. She liked the independence—being able to do whatever she wanted to do whenever she wanted to do it. Always busy with her dancing, she never had time to feel lonely or bored. Until now. Now she had tasted something unlike anything she had ever experienced, and being alone would never be the same again.

Chapter Four

Doc paced back and forth. He hated himself for doing this. It wasn't like him, but he didn't know what else to do. After she left, the choice seemed obvious, and uncomplicated. So he went back. Back home to his mountain. Back to where he grew up and felt comfortable. Despite all his travels and all his education, this place was the only place for him. He had long known that, and it had never seemed like a problem before. But now...Now his world had changed, and for the first time in his life he didn't know what to do. So, confused, he hadn't called her. He just packed his things and left, and now he felt terrible about it. He hadn't been brought up to go back on his word. Honesty was highly valued in the Cove. A man's word was absolute—no other security was needed. Whether buying property or a hog, a man's word and a handshake were good enough.

"Settle down, child! You're a gonna wear a hole clean through this porch!" Granny's dark face wrinkled up even more when she spoke. She wasn't Doc's real grandmother, she was his great aunt. She wasn't anyone's real grandmother, but she was everybody's. She'd been a fixture in the community for as long as anyone could remember, and no one knew exactly how old she was. She herself didn't remember the exact number. If anyone was impertinent enough to ask, she would just cock her head back and laugh.

"Child," she'd say, sweeping her hand across the horizon, "You see that mountain yonder? Well, I'm older than the dirt on *it*." She'd laugh again, and then invite the child to "set a spell and have a peppermint."

She did all the "doctorin" and "birthin" that needed to be done, and always had. There had never been a real doctor in the Cove. If someone should become critically ill, they had to get down the mountain and into town, or wait until the doctor could be sent for. By the time he arrived, it was often too late. The patient had either gotten well or hadn't.

Doc quit pacing. He had come to Granny knowing she was the only one who could help him— if anyone could. He spilled out his story, and she listened to him patiently, her rocking chair thrumping back and forth.

"Come set here." She patted the bench next to her. "Well now. First, and most important, you said you'd call her." She shot him an accusing look over her glasses. "I guess you'd better. Bein' late's better than tellin' tales."

"But I don't know what say to her. I never should have started this whole thing. It was wrong. There's no future for us."

"You don't know that. Things are either going to be, or they're not, and it's not for us to know." She closed her eyes and sighed. She stopped rocking, took off her glasses and spent several minutes cleaning them on her apron before continuing.

"Just tell her the truth, Doc. If she falls in love with you, that's all that'll matter to her. If she is afraid of what you are—well—then you have your answer. And it's an answer you need. Even if it isn't an easy one to hear." She pushed herself up from the chair and walked to the edge of the porch, a sudden breeze ruffling her gray hair.

She smiled. "It's right airish today, Doc. Maybe it will bring good things. Now, go on. You know what you need to do. Time's a wastin'. Take care of your responsibility. So get out of here now and leave me be!" She turned, the screen door banging behind her as she disappeared into the darkness of the house.

He stared after her for a moment. Of course she was right. He knew what he had to do. So he headed back out of the Cove, his hands in his pockets, staring at the hard ground.

****

The weeks of vacation passed, and Hadleigh finally stopped hoping that he would contact her. She settled back into the routine of a new season. The ballet with *Poet's Muse* had been laid to rest in the repertory, to be resurrected at some later date. So that problem was solved, at least for the time being. The cast list for the new season of performances had been posted, and Hadleigh was back doing strictly corps work. Not that it surprised her. It was becoming clear that this was not a good situation for her if she wanted to move up in her career.

Her time with Doc had slowly taken on the quality of a wonderful dream. She knew that was all it would ever be, and she tried to push it out of her mind. Maybe someday the memory of him wouldn't be so painful, but for now it was better ignored. Try as she might, though, he kept creeping back into her thoughts. It was frustrating. Was Jasmine right about him being just another wealthy man with a ballerina obsession? Was that really all there was to it? Or did Hadleigh just not want to believe it wasn't something more?

She heaved her dance bag over her shoulder, ready to head home. Jann walked up and fell in step beside her.

"Hey, how about doing something interesting?"

Hadleigh paused. "Okay, I'll bite. Like what?"

"Like go to the library."

"Wow. Leave it to you to come up with another thrilling adventure. What, pray tell, are we going to do there?"

"Well, I am tired of you moping around, and last night I had this sudden inspiration."

"Go on."

She lowered her voice and feigned a foreign accent. "I think you need closure." She pretended to look out over imaginary spectacles. "I remembered that there is some reference book where you can look up all the doctors in this country, and what their specialty is, etc. So all we have to do is find him in there, and you can contact him—or not—, "she added hastily, "and that will be that."

"I appreciate your efforts, Jann, I really do. But I do not need *closure*, as you so colorfully put it." She stopped and leaned back against the wall.

"Ah," Jann said, pushing at the phantom spectacles again, "I beg to differ."

"I just want to go home, soak in a nice hot tub, and put my feet up."

Jann paused for a moment, disappointed. Then she shrugged, heaved her dance bag up on her shoulder, and added matter-of-factly: "Suit yourself. I guess I'll just see you later, then." She picked up her pace and walked down the stairs and out onto the street.

Hadleigh hesitated and almost started after her, but then she stopped. *Am I really such a basket-case?* Jann usually minded her own business when things got rocky. She knew Hadleigh well enough to know that she preferred to handle whatever problems came along on her own, in a quiet and logical way. So this little intervention was quite a departure. They had been roommates and friends now for more than five years, and this was this first time Jann had made any attempt to give unsolicited advice. Hadleigh couldn't decide if it was a good thing or not. Jann always teased her about her 'inability to flirt' and often offered suggestions in that department, but never something like this.

Hadleigh straightened her shoulders. *I am going to stop wallowing in self-pity right now! If Jann is giving up on me, then I must really be a mess.* She decided to head for that hot bath after all, to symbolically wash him out of her system, once and for all.

It was more than an hour later when Jann returned. She was quiet. Way too quiet, especially for Jann. Hadleigh wondered if she had really hurt her feelings today by nixing the trip to the library.

"Hey, is everything okay with you?" Hadleigh said, breaking the silence. Jann collapsed on the sofa and clicked on the television before answering.

"Yeah."

"I don't believe you." Hadleigh insisted. "Did I say something today I shouldn't have?"

"No, it's not you."

"Well, what is it then?"

Jann muted the volume on the remote and looked at Hadleigh.

"Look, I went to the library anyway. I guess because *I* wanted to know, and so when you changed your mind I could say 'Aha! Here is his phone number!' and you would call him and everything would settle down."

"And we would live happily ever after?"

"No, but *you* would." She sighed and switched off the TV. "Okay, here goes. This is what I uncovered." She took a deep breath. "He's not a doctor. Or, at least, he's not listed in any of the materials the librarian showed me. It looks like Jasmine was right. More than right." She stood up and walked over to Hadleigh. "I'm so sorry."

Hadleigh collapsed on the sofa. She felt like someone had just punched her in the stomach, even though she knew, deep down, what his not calling had meant. But then she felt angry—angry that anyone would go to such lengths just to get a ballerina on their arm.

"Well! I can't believe he would tell such an outrageous lie. I would have gone out with him anyway," she said defiantly.

"Hmmm." Jann murmured. "I don't know if I would have. What if he said he was a dirt salesman from Podunk. A well-spoken, well-dressed, attractive dirt salesman, but a dirt-seller nonetheless. Are you sure you would have called him?"

"Well...maybe not a *dirt salesman*."

"I rest my case."

Hadleigh shifted uncomfortably. Jann was very good at calling things by their true name, and she had called this one. Hadleigh had to admit that the image of a tall, dark, handsome doctor appealed to her highly developed sense of romance. That also explained her heightened attraction to him. Simple as that.

Jann laid the remote on the table. "I'm too tired even for TV. I'm going to bed, and my feet are so sore I'm going to stick them out at the end of the sheets. Tom was brutal in rehearsal today. That last run-through was cruel and unnecessary, and I just hope I can get my pointe shoes on tomorrow without a sledgehammer. Good night." She hobbled off to the bedroom.

Hadleigh grinned in spite of herself. "I agree with you about the sheets and the rehearsal," she called after her, "but I think I will watch some television. Maybe it will put me to sleep." She clicked on the remote and began surfing, hoping to find something, anything, to distract her muddled thoughts. It was well after midnight when she drifted off into an uncomfortable slumber.

****

Hadleigh lay on her back, feet in the air, legs against the wall. It was the only position that kept the blood from pounding through her tender feet. The first weeks of a new season were always hard on toes that had become tender from a few weeks of disuse. But she knew they would toughen up eventually, so when her section of the ballet was not being rehearsed, she just put her feet up on the wall.

It helped, at least for a little while.

She stared up at the ceiling, oblivious to the panting of the dancers in the second section now being run through their paces. She fixed her gaze on a small piece of tape stuck by some fragment of persistence to the overhead plaster, undoubtedly left over from the decorations of some old cast party. She wondered how long it would stick before giving up.

Derek came and flopped down beside her. He was a male principal with the company, likeable, and a born entertainer, onstage or off.

"Whew. I don't know who lit a fire under Tom lately, but these multiple run-throughs are becoming excessive. I am *not* a machine."

"Oh yes you are. That's what we're paid to be, remember?"

"Oh dar-lin'! It's worse than I thought! Our Pollyanna optimist is going down fast!" He poked her with his foot. "Machines, now, are we? Well, then it's time to close shop for the day because the quota of pirouettes has been exhausted."

Derek maintained that every studio had a set quota for certain steps, and once it had been exceeded—say by some dancer doing an unusual number of turns—no one else would be able to pirouette well for the rest of the day.

Hadleigh laughed. Jasmine *had* outdone herself in the pirouette department today, but then, she was known as a "turner." Jann insisted she was just a one-trick pony. Not that Derek ever seemed to be adversely effected by any quotas. An obvious talent, he seemed to find even the most difficult combinations pretty easy. His attitude was easy, too. No affectations or pretensions. He was easy to get along with and seemed to like everyone. Even Jasmine, with whom he was frequently paired.

Derek lay back and closed his eyes. "So, Pollyanna—what's up with you? How's your social life? If you have any free time, I've been thinking about working up a couple of pas de deuxs, and I was wondering if you might be interested."

Hadleigh sat up and folded her feet under her. "What kind of a pas, and for what?"

"Well, there's a little competition coming up— nothing major—just an *international* one, and this year they have a couples section. So I was thinking of entering. Both classical and contemporary pieces are required. So, what do you think? Will your feet hold up for some extracurricular pointe activity?"

"You don't mean *the* International Ballet Competition?" Hadleigh didn't quite consider herself in that league, at least not yet. He had to be kidding. Sometimes it was hard to tell with Derek. "Boy, you *are* overworked," she added.

He sat up and stared at her. "No, seriously. I think you would be perfect. You have the technique, but most of all, you have the *artistry*. For a couple's competition that is essential. I'm asking you to be my partner, in all seriousness. So, are you game?"

Hadleigh hesitated. Just moments before, she had been toying with the idea of giving it all up and doing something—anything—else for a living. And now this. She looked at him and said simply, "Okay."

"Great! I thought we'd start with the pas from *Giselle*. How do you feel about that? We can decide later what the other ones should be."

"That's great! I've always wanted to do that pas. Who will be coaching us?"

"Adam volunteered. He thinks we have a good shot at it."

Wow. Hadleigh hadn't expected that. Apparently there were more things going on behind her back and behind the scenes than she imagined.

"I hope you don't mind rehearsing on Sundays, at least at first. It's the only time we can snag a free studio."

Hadleigh stifled a groan. Sunday was the only day off they had every week, and it was always difficult to get everything done in that one day, like laundry and grocery shopping. Nonetheless, she wasn't going to give up this opportunity that had dropped out of the sky.

"I don't mind. As long it doesn't take the whole day."

"No problem. I have to do laundry, too." He smiled and stood up. "You're going to be wonderful, dar-lin."

Hadleigh smiled. "Thanks!"

Derek just waved and sauntered off toward the dressing rooms, since Tom had finally called it a day. Hadleigh sat for a moment trying to let it sink in. The International Competition? Did she really have a chance of even placing? She must, or else Adam wouldn't have offered to be their coach. She had always dreamed of being good enough to compete in the international arena, and now that it was happening she could hardly believe it! Her enthusiasm returned in an instant. Yes, Adam wouldn't have agreed if he didn't believe she had a shot, because it meant a large time commitment from him, too. Plus, he would have to travel with them and work extra hours, so it would cut deeply into his personal time.

She stripped off her pointe shoes. Ahh. Freedom at last. She wiggled her toes, looked up, and almost fainted. The room had emptied of dancers anxious to get home, and she was alone. Except for the large, handsome man standing in the doorway.

"Hi. They said up front it was okay to come back since you were finished for the day. I hope you don't mind." Doc shifted back and forth on his feet, looking out of place as usual.

"Doc." Hadleigh, still in shock, felt her pulse racing. "What are you doing here?"

"I couldn't stay away. I had to see you...talk to you again."

Hadleigh began to regain her senses. "Oh. I see."

She tried not to notice how blue his eyes looked in this light, or how broad and strong his chest appeared under his dark shirt.

"I am sorry I didn't call. It was a terrible thing to do—to disappear like I did. But if you will hear me out, I'd like to explain. Or try to." He brushed that wayward lock of hair back. "There are a great many things I would like to explain, as a matter of fact."

Hadleigh walked deliberately past him and toward the dressing room. "Let me get dressed and get my things. There is something I want to say to you, too."

"Alright. I'll just wait for you in the lobby."

"Fine."

She collapsed on the bench in front of the mirror and stared at her reflection. Was it a full moon today? Or was she dreaming? No, this felt altogether too real to be a dream, and the pounding in her feet lent credence to the whole scenario. She knew exactly what piece of her mind she was going to give Doc for lying to her about being a doctor, and for not calling her like he said he would. But hesitation crept into her resolve. She wasn't sure how to proceed. What did he really want from her? Did he just happen to be in town and need an arm piece for the evening? Or had he really come just to see her? She didn't know what to think or whether to believe him.

She got dressed, threw her things into her dance bag, and strode down the hall. No, it wasn't a dream. He was still there.

He started to take her bag from her, but she pulled it back. "I can manage, thank you."

"I don't blame you for being angry. But you must have met many men who promised to call you and didn't. Isn't that true?"

"That doesn't make it right."

"Absolutely. And I do apologize. Sincerely." He

looked at her again with that intensity she found so hard to resist. "Now may I carry your bag for you? I hate it when I am not allowed to be a gentleman."

Hadleigh hesitated, then released her hold. He slipped the bag easily onto his shoulder despite it being full of several pairs of shoes, changes of clothes, make-up, hair spray, adhesive tape, a full water bottle, plus various and sundry other supplies.

"Is there a place we can go to talk that's private and restful? I'm not used to big city life. I'd really like to see a tree or two. Or three or four."

Hadleigh thought for a moment, wrinkling her brow in a way that was a peculiar combination of child and woman. "Oh, yes! I know the perfect place." She nodded, her face lighting up. "It's in Central Park."

"Isn't that where people get mugged all the time?" He teased. "Are you planning to get rid of me that way?"

"Well, I *had* thought about it, but my hired thugs have the rest of the week off." She smiled. "Actually, the place I have in mind is a local secret the tourists haven't discovered yet. I think it will meet with your approval. But it's a pretty good walk. Would you rather take the bus?"

"Is it less than ten miles?"

Hadleigh laughed. "Quite!"

"Then I'd rather walk. Unless, of course, you'd prefer a rest after dancing all day."

Suddenly Hadleigh didn't feel tired at all—quite the contrary. "I'd rather walk, too. I hate the bus. Too noisy and crowded."

So walk they did. She fell easily into step with him, and for a long while they were both silent. Then Doc said, "I'd like to hear more about what makes someone choose to be a dancer. It seems like a pretty iffy profession in a lot of ways. You seem to have some fame, but not fortune, and the fame seems to be rather peculiar and limited. Otherwise you couldn't dine freely at old dime stores—or need to. It's not like being a movie star."

"That's true." Hadleigh nodded pensively. "One of my favorite quotes is from Margot Fonteyn. She was a famous dancer from England, and lots of books have been written about her. She said in one of them that being a dancer is like 'coming out into the spotlight, and walking home in the rain.' I think that sums it up pretty well. Anyone who goes into dance for fame and fortune is misguided."

"But there must be other perks."

"Oh yes. The fame may be limited, but it's not bad. The people who follow the ballet love it—and us. They are always kind with their compliments and support. Best of all are the children. We are the dancers they dream about becoming, although I sometimes have mixed feelings about encouraging them to take it up as a career. It is demanding, and it doesn't leave much time for anything else. I teach a children's class at the company school anyway, and I enjoy it. The students are so motivated and optimistic." Then her expression sobered. "I want to give them some positive experiences in ballet before the optimism is slowly beaten out of them."

"Does that really happen?"

"Not always. But the philosophy of training dancers is not unlike military training, and it all begins around the tender age of eight. Teachers are supposed to ignore the things students do well and ride them mercilessly about their mistakes. The belief—the tradition—is that dancers won't work hard if they are praised too much."

"Then why would anyone *choose* to do it?"

"I've asked myself that a million times. I have no idea. Maybe because we like a challenge? Or maybe we're just a bunch of masochistic fools." She smiled mischievously.

Then, unable to hold it in any longer, Hadleigh blurted it out. "Why did you lie to me about being a doctor? Did you really think you had to put on such a charade to get my attention?"

Blindsided, Doc stopped and stared at her.

"I have *never* put on a charade to get anyone's attention. I never would. And I *did not* lie to you."

"But you're not in any reference book that lists doctors," Hadleigh confessed, feeling her cheeks start to burn. "So could you explain that, please?"

Doc raised his eyebrows, and smiled. "So you tried to check up on me, did you?" He began walking his steady pace again.

"Well...sort of." She fell in beside him.

"Hmmm. Of course you know there are many different kinds of doctors, not just medical specialists. How about people with doctoral degrees in education or biology? Did you rule me out as one of those too?"

"Well...not exactly." She began to feel pretty small all of a sudden, forgetting that he *had* lied when he said he would call her.

Then he let out a low whistle. They approached the Conservatory Garden, and it was beautiful. The sidewalk was bordered on each side with flowering trees that had spilled their blossoms earthward, so the concrete was heavily dusted in pink hues. The park benches, from the 1939 World's Fair, were artistic and unusual, with curved arms and legs.

"You certainly picked a lovely spot." He brushed some petals off of a bench. "Shall we sit here? It looks like a suitable spot for revealing secrets and truths."

She looked at him, feeling uncomfortable. He just smiled. A little sadly, she thought. Hadleigh sat down and brushed some more petals off the armrest. He sat down beside her, but not too close this time.

He cleared his throat and shifted on the bench. "This is kind of a long story, but you need to hear all of it in order to understand." He pushed his hair back and settled his gaze on her face. "You are guilty in this, too. You never asked me anything about my being a doctor. Not what my specialty was or even where I practiced. You just assumed everything. I would have been happy to answer any questions you had." He paused and moved his body a bit closer to her, then reached up to her face and caressed her cheek, running two fingers gently down it. He lowered his voice, almost to a whisper. "But I let you assume. I knew what you thought, and I let you believe it because it made you happy. It was what you wanted to believe. I knew, even then, that what I wanted more than anything else was to make you happy."

Hadleigh blushed. "Doc..."

"Shhh." He slid closer and put his fingers over her lips. "There is so much I need to say, and a lot of it may not make you happy. But I have to tell you the truth."

Hadleigh nodded, her eyes fixed on him.

"I am not a doctor, I am a schoolteacher. I work in a remote—a very, very remote—community in the mountains of North Carolina. There are no roads leading to it. You have to take a train or walk the tracks three and a half miles to the foot of the mountain. From there you must walk a steep, rocky trail more than a mile to get to the top." He shifted his position and placed his hand on hers, caressing it lightly. "I was born into a large family. I have—had—six brothers and two sisters. It is my home, a part of me, and I cannot ever leave it for good. I am needed there—desperately. As much as any medical doctor, and there have been many times I wished I was one." He paused, his expression clouding. "My parents are both long dead, and only four of my six brothers survive." He paused. "Are you beginning to see why I decided to run from you?"

Hadleigh looked into his face. "Go on."

He stared off into space for a moment, and Hadleigh wondered where his thoughts were taking him, his expression was so strange.

"I guess you're wondering why anyone would choose to live in such isolation. It all started long, long before my time, when some of my ancestors fled into the hills and discovered our Cove. It was a long time ago. Back when the Constitution was changed. Back when anyone listed as a free person of color was no longer allowed to own land." He paused a moment, trying to judge her reaction.

Hadleigh looked at him, her eyes widening. Of course—the tanned skin, the dark hair. It began to make sense. Surely he didn't think that would make any difference to her.

He turned his gaze away and continued. "My ancestors came to the mountains to hide, to be left alone, and, as Granny tells it, to be unmolested by the town folk until we could, over the generations, become 'white enough.' Or until society itself changed. Some people call us Melungeons. But since that term is sometimes—yes, even now—used as a term of scorn, many of us never use it. But you will hear it. That is, if you spend any time with me. Back when my brothers and I were small, we were seldom allowed to go down the mountain and into town because my parents wanted to protect us from the things we might hear people say. But when we got older, we were needed to help bring supplies back up into the Cove, so we began going along. My mother developed a secret signaling system for us. If she wanted us to wait and be quiet, she would squeeze our hand once. If she wanted us to follow her, she'd squeeze twice. My favorite one was the three squeeze signal, because that meant, 'I...love...you.' One squeeze for each word. She used it often. Anytime she needed to say it, or thought we needed to hear it, but didn't want to embarrass us by saying it out loud."

"She sounds like a special person."

He just nodded and stared at the ground for

several minutes. Hadleigh waited, wondering why any of this would make a difference to her and the way she felt about him.

Doc shifted on the bench, easing into his story. "Have you heard of my people before?"

"No," Hadleigh said, "I haven't. Who are they—I mean—you?"

"Some people say we are a mystery race. The Lost Tribe of Israel. Some say we are a tri-racial group of Caucasian, Native American and African American. Some say we are the descendants of the Lost Colony of Roanoke. I have heard from some of my relatives that we were descended from the Portuguese, or, as they put it—Portyghee. The truth is, no one really knows. It is probably lost forever in history. But the fact is, those of us who looked white, and passed for white on the census, were able to own property. Those who didn't—well—they went into the hills. Deep and far into the hills, where they stayed. Today most of them wouldn't know how to live any other way. There are, right now, eight families spread throughout the Cove, and twenty-four children of various ages in my school." He paused and stared off into the distance. Then he said, almost to himself, "It's only through the children that there can be any hope of changing the way the world is, and for them to do that, they need an education, a good solid education that covers more than reading and writing."

"And that's where you come in, and why you can't leave."

"Right."

"I see." Hadleigh brushed more petals off her lap. "I guess I do understand why you wanted to disappear, but you could have told me all of this earlier. It wouldn't have changed anything."

"I know I should have, but I was not thinking clearly. And I blame that entirely on you." He smiled and slipped his arm around her shoulders. "But I want you to know that's not my usual way of operating."

Hadleigh tried to ignore the distracting warmth of his arm around her and said, "What I'd like to know now is why you changed your mind. Why did you come back here to find me?"

He looked at her for a while before answering then took her hand again. "I couldn't stop thinking about you. I missed everything about you, right down to the sound of your voice." He slid even closer to her. "I didn't know what else to do, and now that I'm here, I still don't know what to do."

"Wait a minute." Hadleigh pulled her hand away. "If you're not a doctor, then why do you go around telling people you are, and have everyone call you 'Doc'?"

"As I told you before, I *never* said I was a doctor." He reached for her hand again. "But it *is* my name. My true, legal, baptized name. There is a tradition—I don't know where it came from—of naming a seventh son in any family 'Doctor.' You see it often in mountain families, going back many generations. Perhaps it's related to a belief in the number seven being lucky. I don't know." He paused, and looked at her, his gaze skimming over her face. Hadleigh felt a shiver go up her spine. "But I do know I *never* should have deceived you, even indirectly. I should have set you straight right away. For that I am very sorry. I wasn't raised that way."

"Well, I suppose I did sort of jump to that conclusion, but you *certainly* helped it along. I guess that kind of misunderstanding must happen to you a lot. You must get tired of explaining."

"Goes with the territory. It has been my experience that people believe what they want to believe about someone, both good and bad things. Especially if it feeds into their prejudices..." he inclined his head and looked at her directly "...or their fantasies." With a gentle touch he pulled her to face him and leaned his face close to hers. "So, am I now forgiven?" he whispered.

Hadleigh lowered her glance. "I guess so."

"I can't get anything better than that?" He curved his fingers under her chin and lifted it, bringing her face closer to his. She closed her eyes and gave in to the warm, delicious pressure of his lips. And in it, Doc knew he'd found his answer. His kiss grew deeper and more insistent, lasting long after a breeze came up, causing swirls of petals to dance around them.

Chapter Five

It was late when Hadleigh came home, and Jann was there waiting for her.

"Well!? What's the scoop?"

"Jann, I am the happiest unhappy person in the world tonight." She collapsed on the sofa. "Can I give you details tomorrow? My brain is so muddled now, I can't think straight."

"Aaaarrrgh! Why must you put your best friend through such agony?" She shuffled back to her room. "Well, it better be good tomorrow! Good night!" She called back over her shoulder.

"'Night," Hadleigh turned off the light and stared out the window into the city. She had been so excited about the upcoming competition and what it might mean to her career. But right now it seemed to pale in the scheme of things. She thought about Doc. Could they make a long-distance relationship work? If so, for how long? She knew she couldn't give up something she had worked her whole life for, nor, apparently, could he. So at least they understood each other. For all the good it did. Hadleigh sighed and resolved to be Scarlett again. I'll worry about all this tomorrow. With that, she crawled into bed and slept. And dreamed. Dreamed of running with Doc, barefoot and laughing, through fields covered in pink petals. In a beautiful world, so covered in mist it was hard to see him at times. Then he would appear again, laughing, running, holding his arms open to her, bidding her to come to him...to follow him...to follow him...

****

The day dawned gray and rainy, as gray as only

New York can be—lingering, oppressive, and all encompassing. The lights of the buildings made a fierce but futile attempt to brighten the day. Doc paced back and forth in his hotel room, occasionally glancing out the window to the slick black streets below. He wondered how she could stand it here. So few green, growing things. He knew he could never survive here, and he felt a cold fear creep around his heart. He wondered if she could ever live anywhere else. Even if she tried to, would she hate it? Would she end up hating him? She had told him about the upcoming competition, and the excitement in her eyes told him all he needed to know and didn't really want to hear. He hadn't known what to expect when he came here, but now he realized what he had hoped for. That she would want to leave this place someday, and he could take her to his world—his beautiful, green, sweet-smelling world—and she would love it as much as he did. But deep inside he knew there was no way this could work. He couldn't expect her to give up her life. It wouldn't be fair, and it would make everything too difficult for both of them. His decision made, he stopped pacing and picked up the phone.

Hadleigh heard it ringing when she was halfway down the stairs, so she sprinted back and picked it up.

"Hello?"

"Hi. I hoped I'd catch you. There's been a change in plans and I have to leave tonight. Is there any chance I can see you before I go?"

Hadleigh caught her breath. She noticed he had become awfully quiet last night during the taxi ride back to her apartment. "Oh, Doc—I don't know. I have rehearsals scheduled all day long, with only a short lunch break. I'm also required to be at a company fund-raising reception tonight until late."

"How about if I bring us a lunch and we find a quiet place to share it?"

"Okay. I finish my first rehearsal at twelve-thirty."

"I'll see you then."

Finding a quiet, private place at the ballet studio presented a definite challenge. It was still pouring outside, so slipping outdoors was out of the question. Because of the weather, most of the dancers stayed inside instead of going out to eat. Hadleigh decided they would just have to settle for a corner of the lobby and hope for the best.

She waited there for him, and soon he breezed in the door, shaking off his umbrella as he entered. Seeing him caused her heart to skip a beat, but by now she was getting used to that. He carried two paper bags and a small bouquet of flowers. Mercifully, the dancers who had settled in another corner got up and made themselves scarce.

"Something to brighten up this day." He smiled and handed them to her. "Although you do a pretty good job all by yourself."

Hadleigh blushed. "I'm sorry I couldn't arrange more private accommodations—but please, have a seat." She motioned to the old couch that sagged in the middle from years of use by the famous and the hopeful.

He dug out the cartons and set up their lunch on small coffee table.

"I hope you like Chinese. It seemed to be the easiest thing to handle in this weather. Small white cartons with handles, and all. Would you prefer your fried rice with shrimp or beef?"

"It doesn't matter. I like both."

"Well then, perhaps we should share."

Hadleigh sat down beside him, but her appetite seemed to have left her. She had a bad feeling in the pit of her stomach, as though she could sense what was coming.

"What's happened to make you leave so soon? I was hoping to have a chance to show you more of the city. Things I'm sure you would like."

"You're the only thing I care about seeing."

She blushed again. Why was he saying these things now that he was getting ready to leave? She didn't know how to respond. Her feelings had become so intense they frightened her.

"You still didn't tell me why you have to leave so soon."

"Because I must. You have a life here that you love. I don't want to be the one who..." He stopped. Hadleigh's eyes were fixed on him, her expression puzzled. She was unreadable. Did he detect something there? Or was it just something he wanted to find? And what if he did? She didn't seem fazed by his background, only upset about his leading her astray about his name. He was more confused than before.

"The one who what?" She pleaded.

He sighed, his convictions evaporating. "Nothing. Maybe I have been too hasty. I guess I can stay long enough for you to show me the sights. It sounds like you have something in mind."

"Well, there are lots of things. I know you would like to see more of Central Park. Maybe that would be a good start. If not, I know lots of wonderful restaurants. Or I could entertain you by showing you my apartment. It's so tiny Jann says you have to go outside to change your mind."

He smiled. "Is Jann the girl you were with at the restaurant?"

"Yes..."

"And the one who put you up to sending me the refill?"

Hadleigh dropped her focus to the floor and nodded.

"I had a feeling. Now I have a confession. I thought you two were—how shall I say this—making fun of me? You see, I jumped to that conclusion because I have—sometimes—been treated poorly by some people in my area because of being Melungeon. Would you believe some of the town people actually try to scare their children by saying, 'the Melungeons will get you if you don't behave'?"

Hadleigh gasped. That sounded like something out of the history books. She didn't think things like that happened today. She said softly, "I'm so sorry, I had no idea."

"Well, the waitress set me straight when I went back there that evening. She had been listening to you two talking, and I guess thought it was the sweetest thing in the world. So of course she let me know about you all being dancers with the company that was in town, and the rest, as they say, is history."

"Ah...it all makes sense now." Hadleigh glanced up at the clock. "Uh oh...I have to be in rehearsal in two minutes." She started to gather up the remnants of lunch.

"You go ahead. I'll take care of this, providing you tell me when I can get that tour of Central Park."

"Well, tomorrow is my off day." Then she remembered. "Oh no! I promised to rehearse for the competition on Sundays. But I'll be finished by the afternoon, if that isn't too late?"

"Shall I come by here, or should I get a tour of your miniature apartment beforehand?"

"I guess tours will be the order of the day. Why don't you come by about three—I'm at two thirty-four West Forty-ninth Street, Apartment fifty-two."

"Three it is."

She stood up and said, "Oh yes, I should warn you. It's on the fifth floor, and there are no elevators. It's a walk-up."

He laughed. "I think I can handle it."

He wanted to kiss her but the lobby and hall were suddenly teeming with bodies. So, he just smiled at her and let himself out.

****

Derek was already on the floor stretching when she arrived at the studio on Sunday afternoon. It was a beautiful day, one made for enjoying the outdoors. But they had things to do and places to go, as Derek so succinctly put it.

"Hi, darlin'! Are you ready for fame and fortune on the international stage?" He teased, looking in the mirror and fluffing up his blond hair.

"Absolutely. I'm lining up interviews now."

"As well you should be." He grinned. "Adam should be here in a few minutes, but if you don't mind, I'd like a chance to try some things before he gets here." He stood up, stretching his arms behind his back. "But I'll let you get warmed up first. I'll be in the video room. I brought an old tape of Makarova and Nagy doing Giselle. I thought it would be some good inspiration."

"Great. I'd like to see it, too, sometime."

Hadleigh put on her pointe shoes and walked over to the barre. She began doing pliés and tendus. Their soothing repetition eased both body and mind into the routine. Yet she couldn't help looking a little bit longingly out the window. Ah, well, three o'clock would get here soon enough.

Giselle was one of Hadleigh's favorite ballets, with its romantic story of a young peasant girl betrayed by her lover. She dies and becomes a Wili, the ghost of a girl who dies before her wedding day. The pas de deux they would be rehearsing was from the second act, when Giselle's lover comes to her gravesite, and she appears—to save him from the other Wilis who are determined to force him to dance until he dies. She dances with him throughout the night, helping him when he falters. When dawn breaks, the Wili's power is no more and Giselle disappears with them, having succeeded in saving her lover's life.

It was an unusual choice for a competition.

Although technically demanding, it was not the usual bravura showpiece. It was, however, well suited to Hadleigh and Derek's abilities. They both knew the choreography well. It was traditional, and they had done it before in various pas de deux classes, although never before with each other. So it was just a matter of polishing it and getting used to working it together.

Hadleigh had just finished warming up when Adam strode into the room. Never one to waste time, he said, "Hello people. Are we ready to go? Shall we just walk through it once, for timing?"

Hadleigh nodded and Derek sprinted in. The music started. Its haunting quality washed over her. It made her feel like Giselle—ethereal, other-worldly, and sad. They marked through the steps with ease. She and Derek fit together well; their timing was similar, and he had no problem at all matching her line and artistry.

Adam nodded his approval. "Let's try a full run-through and see where the problems are going to be."

The music started again, and they went at it full-out. The most difficult part for Hadleigh was the opening. A solo adagio, it contained several tricky balances and promenades. The actual partnering went well, with only a few baubles on one lift. They finished, flushed with perspiration.

"Well." Adam cleared his throat. "Hadleigh, we need to get you a little more secure on that opening, but other than that...well, it's amazing. You two fit together beautifully. Of course, we need to talk about what other pieces you'll be doing, since it looks like this one won't be much of a problem. I'd considered something like *Esmeralda,* for the contrast. I also thought about *Don Q*, but it's been done to death. Then there are a couple of more modernistic pieces I've wanted to choreograph, and that would cover the contemporary requirements. In fact, if you don't mind staying a bit longer today, we could get started on it."

Hadleigh's heart dropped. A dancer would *never* to say to her director, "Oh, so sorry, but I have another engagement." Especially under these circumstances—when Adam was giving up his Sunday to coach them, and time was short. So, swallowing hard she said, "That's fine, I just need to make a phone call."

Adam nodded and busied himself with the CD player.

In the lobby, Hadleigh dialed Doc's room. No answer. She let it ring a long time, in case he was in the shower or something, but still nothing. Changing tactics, she rang her apartment.

"Hello."

"Jann, it's me. I have to stay longer than expected and I can't reach Doc. He's coming by about three. I'll get there as soon as I can."

"Wow! I finally get to entertain Dr. Milk. How exciting! Any information you want me to extract from him? It can be arranged."

"Thanks, but that won't be necessary. Just let him know that this was beyond my control, and I'll be there as soon as I can."

"Will do."

****

In the throes of his creativity, Adam let the rehearsal drag on and on. Hadleigh tried not to watch the clock and forced herself to concentrate on the choreography. The piece was going to be great. A fun, light comedy, it was another unusual choice for a competition, but something that might work well. On any other day, Hadleigh would have been excited by the creative challenge it provided; but as the minutes ticked by, she became more and more desperate. Finally, Adam called a five-minute break, and she dashed to the phone. It was 4:15.

Quickly she rang her apartment.

"Hi. It's me again. He's still got us working. Can I speak with Doc, please?"

Jann said, "Hadleigh, he just left. He's going to meet you there. Oh yes, one other thing. He *is* charming. You lucky dog! I almost decided to steal him away. You can't let him out of your sight for too long, not the way he looks! Better be careful! Now, don't let Adam keep you there all night. You need some personal time."

Hadleigh walked back into the studio, and found Adam and Derek engaged in a solemn conversation.

"Come on over. You need to hear this too." Derek motioned her over.

Adam cleared his throat. "I was just telling Derek that it would be better for you not to mention these rehearsals to anyone—especially Jasmine. You see, she would like to be doing it, and I just don't want to start anything right now."

"But she's going to find out!" Hadleigh protested. "Why not just be open about it now?"

Adam shook his head. "Trust me, it's better this way. Once things get going, it will be too late for her to say anything, and I can take care of things then. But for now, please don't say anything. Okay?"

Hadleigh reluctantly sighed an 'okay' under her breath. It was all crystal clear now. No wonder they had to rehearse on Sunday. No wonder Adam was more pressed for time than seemed necessary. He always had been the butt of company gossip for being hen-pecked by his wife, but this really took the cake.

"Okay, I guess that's enough for today," Adam finally caved. "Do you two think you could come in a little earlier next Sunday?"

"Sure." Derek agreed.

"I guess so." Hadleigh said, but without enthusiasm.

Adam gave her a sharp glance. "You *do* want to do this? I mean *really* want to do this? Because you have to—or it's pointless. If you have any doubts, tell me *now*. Jasmine will be more than happy to take your place."

Hadleigh bristled at the mention of Jasmine. She straightened up and responded, "Oh no! Of course I really want it! I'm just a little tired today, that's all."

"Good girl! I thought I'd been right about you. Now get out of here and go get some rest." He turned on his heel and left the studio.

No sooner had he disappeared than Doc appeared in the doorway.

"Can I watch? Or is it forbidden without a ticket?" He smiled that wonderful uplifting smile. Hadleigh's fatigue vanished in an instant.

Derek chimed in. "It's not forbidden, but we're finished for the day. *Finally.*" Derek winked at her. "Aren't you going to introduce us?"

"Oh, of course. Derek, this is my friend Doc. Doc, Derek." They shook hands, and as Derek turned his back to Doc, he mouthed the word 'Wow,' before disappearing into the dressing room.

"I am *so* sorry. This was kind of an unusual situation," Hadleigh apologized.

"Well, I hoped that this isn't the way you dancers operate. I *have* heard rumors that you all think dance is the only thing in the world. I was afraid I'd been forgotten in the passion of the moment." He looked at her a little sadly and she knew he was only half-kidding. "I did enjoy meeting your roommate and fellow conspirator. She is quite a live-wire, but she seems nice," he added. He studied her face, noticing that she appeared pretty tired. "Are you still up for Central Park? I already got the five cent tour of your apartment."

"Absolutely. Just let me shower and change, and I'll be right with you." Hadleigh dashed out of the studio and down the hall.

****

Central Park was beautiful, and the day, although waning, was still perfect. Hadleigh and Doc walked around a long time, sometimes talking, sometimes just enjoying the comfortable silence between them. Doc sensed by now she must be feeling beyond tired, so he asked, "Have you ever taken one of the carriage rides? It looks like fun, but perhaps for you it would be old hat."

"No, not at all. I would love to! Believe or not, I have never taken one. Dancers don't get out much, you know." She smiled.

Doc looked down at her upturned face and marveled again at the mix of innocence and worldliness there. He wasn't sure if she was teasing about not getting out much. He suspected there was more truth than jest in her statement. She appeared to live a somewhat cloistered life, but so did he, isolated as he was up in the mountains.

As if by magic, a carriage appeared around the bend. They walked toward it, and it stopped in front of them. Doc helped her up and then swung in beside her. The driver clucked to his horse, and off they went, lulled by the steady clop clop clop of the horse's hooves on the pavement. Although it wasn't cold, a breeze had picked up, so Doc opened out the lap robe and spread it over them. He put his arm around Hadleigh, and she snuggled in closer to him, allowing her head to lean against his shoulder. He reached his other hand under the blanket and took her hand. She felt him squeeze it. Once, twice...three times. She looked up at him, but he appeared to be engrossed in the scenery. Was it an accident? Or did he mean it to be a message to her? She wasn't sure, but she decided to return it anyway. Hesitating only a moment, she squeezed his hand. Three times. She heard his breath catch as he looked down at her, a mixture of disbelief and joy flickering across his face. Then he gathered her into his arms and kissed her. Not gently this time, but hard and long, until everything, even the rhythmic clop clop clop, faded into oblivion.

****

Darkness began to envelop them by the time Doc helped her down out of the carriage and they started to walk back to her apartment. He held her hand now, and she no longer tried to resist.

Suddenly, surprising even himself, Doc said, "Has anyone ever asked you to give up your dancing? And what would you say if someone were to ask it? This is hypothetical, of course, but would you ever consider it?" There, he said it. It was out in the open. But right away, he was sorry.

Hadleigh gasped and jerked her hand away. "You're *not* being hypothetical. I don't buy that for a second. Give it all up? And do what? Come with you? Or anyone? *Hypothetically?*" She stopped and glared at him. "I don't really know you at all." Trembling and surprised at the intensity of her outburst, she stared down at the sidewalk.

He shook his head. "I'm sorry. You're right. I wasn't being hypothetical. I guess I don't know what I mean, either. Not really." He grabbed her arm to stop her as she began walking a steady pace ahead of him. "All I know is I haven't been able to stop thinking about you. I know it's crazy, but I hoped...well...I hoped it might have been the same for you. That's why I came here, to find out. I am not usually at a loss for words, nor do I usually go chasing about the country after a female."

She stopped and looked up at him, seeing the sincerity in his face. She fought against the moistness creeping into her eyes, and her resistance melted. "You really mean it, don't you? You're not just someone who wants a ballerina on his arm?"

"I want *you* on my arm. I don't care if you're a ballerina or an undertaker."

She smiled in spite of everything.

"Hadleigh, what I came here to say, and have

been hesitant to say, is...I have fallen in love with you. I know it's too soon to say it, and you're right. We hardly know each other. But I hoped—prayed—that I saw the same thing in your eyes."

She looked at him and nodded. "I tried not to think about you, but it kept happening. I thought I would never see you again. I decided you were just another man with a ballerina fantasy." She lowered her head and said, barely above a whisper, "I think I love you too, Doc, and it scares me."

"It scares me, too. Once I arrived here today, I decided not to tell you. I planned to disappear again, this time for good. It seemed like the best thing for both of us. To stop this now, before we could hurt each other." He paused, brushing his hair back out of his face. "So now what do we do? I promise I will never—*never*—ask you to give up something you love so much. I don't know how we can make this work. But if you love me, we have to try. Somehow we must figure out a lot of things ..." He paused, and took a deep breath. "For starters, when are you free to come and visit my place in the world? I would like to show you where, and how, I live. Because you're right. You don't know much about me, and you need to." The tone of his voice changed abruptly, and he stopped walking. "There are many things you need to know, and a great many problems we have to solve if we want this to work."

****

Later that evening, in Hadleigh's apartment, Doc murmured close to her ear, "I really do have to leave in the morning. I can't stay away from my teaching too long, you know. Can I entice you to visit my piece of the world? When do you have any time off?"

"This season ends in a little over a month. I could come then."

"It's all set, then. If you'll fly into Johnson City, Tennessee, I'll pick you up from there. I'll be calling you in between times so we can discuss the details."

"Promises, promises!" Hadleigh teased, but this time she knew he meant it.

"I can't call often. There are no phones in the Cove. I have to go down the mountain to get to a phone. I told you, it's a different way of life."

"What about a cell phone?"

Doc hesitated. "The mountains block the signal. They are useless to us."

"Don't you ever worry about an emergency?"

He said simply, "We live the way we have always lived." He stood up in one fluid movement and Hadleigh followed him to the door. "You need to know all about my world. It's a way of life I cannot leave. Not ever. Please understand. You need to see what sort of baggage I have, and you would inherit, if we ever decide to be together. I am afraid—very much afraid—that it may be asking too much of you." He put his hands gently on her face, and Hadleigh felt their strength. He looked down at her and said, "Even when I don't call, I'll still be thinking of you. Even if we never end up together, I will still think of you. Always."

Hadleigh felt a lump rising in her throat. "I'll be thinking of you, too. Much more than I should."

"I need you to think about what a life with me would mean—*really mean*—for both of us. We need to find a way to work out the needs and desires we each have. We have a lot of thinking to do."

He brushed away the tears that began to fall despite her best efforts. Then he kissed her again, holding her body close to his. So close she felt his heart pounding like it was her own. Doc held her a long time before he reluctantly released her from his embrace. Then he turned, and without a backward glance, disappeared down the stairs.

Chapter Six

Hadleigh entered the dance building the next Sunday with a heavy heart, and working on her one day off didn't help her state of mind. But she did like the Sunday atmosphere. It was quiet, without the usual chaos of people coming and going. At least she could hear herself think, which was good if she could just keep her thoughts on the choreography.

Hadleigh walked down the hall and stepped into the dressing room. Just as she dropped her bag down on the counter, the door slammed behind her, and she jumped in spite of herself. There stood Jasmine, who had, for some unknown reason, been behind the door when Hadleigh walked in.

"Oh! I'm so sorry," Jasmine lied, "I didn't mean to startle you."

"It's okay. I like a good adrenaline rush every now and then." Hadleigh dared not ask the obvious question of *what are you doing here?*

"You didn't really think this was a secret thing you and Derek were doing—did you?" Jasmine spoke without looking at Hadleigh. She gazed at herself in the mirror. Without waiting for an answer, she continued on. "I do hope you don't mind sharing your rehearsal space, since I will be entering the same competition." With deft fingers, she began coiling her heavy ponytail into a bun.

"I never intended it to be a secret, and no, I don't mind sharing." Hadleigh said. "But perhaps we should work out a schedule, so we don't have to share the same hours."

"Oh yes, of course." A knock on the door interrupted, and Hadleigh, assuming it was Derek, went to open it.

There stood Vaslav, famous Russian defector and gold medalist four years ago in the previous international competition. Handsome and charming, he was powerful dancer, who possessed an added talent for self-promotion. He managed to find time not only to dance, but also to act in Hollywood movies, and produce his own line of products from perfume to dancewear. Known only by his first name, Vaslav was famous to more than balletomanes.

"Am I early?" The Russian accent was still apparent, despite his living in America for more than ten years. He still looked eighteen, with his boyish face and athletic build. Women swooned over him, and he took full advantage of it.

"Oh no," Jasmine's voice dripped sugar, "you're perfect." She started out the door, but stopped and added as an afterthought, "Oh. This is my friend, Hadleigh. She's going to be in the competition, too."

"So nice to meet pretty friend." He reached out and shook her hand. "I wish you luck in the competition."

"Thank you." Hadleigh's mind raced. How had Jasmine pulled it off? Vaslav wasn't associated with the company. He wasn't really associated with any company. He preferred to freelance as an individual artist. How had Jasmine managed to get him to partner her, and what chance did she have against this sort of competition? It didn't seem quite fair somehow, but she wasn't sure exactly how.

She walked into the studio and scuffled her feet around in the rosin box. Rosin, or "magic turnout powder" as Derek called it, is the sticky substance that dancers use to gain traction and prevent slipping on polished floors. It is also used during exercises at the barre to insure a solid footing, and to anchor one's feet in a turned-out position. Hadleigh stepped out of the box and came to stand next to

Derek in the corner.

"I see you've met our interlopers," he said soberly. "Well, we'll just have to show them how it's supposed to be done." He grinned at Hadleigh and added, "You're not going to let this get in your way, I hope."

"No, but it was quite a surprise. Do you know how she managed it?"

"Yeah, she knew him when he first came to this country, before she married Adam." He smirked. "You can use your imagination from there. It was back when they were both young and starving. I use the term 'starving' loosely," he added sarcastically.

Very loosely. Vaslav had never been remotely close to starving. There had always been people more than willing to hire him and help him, both in New York and Hollywood.

Jasmine was already out on the floor, and Vaslav soon joined her. Right away it became apparent what one of their selections would be. They were practicing excerpts from *Black Swan*, supposedly the most difficult pas de deux in the classical repertoire. And, Hadleigh had to admit to herself as she watched; they did it extremely well, even this early in the rehearsal process.

"Quit watching them," Derek chided, poking her in the ribs, "and let's go over on the side. We can work on some things while they're warming up."

They began working on the opening of *Giselle*. With its initial developpés and promenades, it didn't require much room. But Jasmine had other ideas.

Adam came into the studio and she confronted him. "I can't work with all that distraction behind me. Could you *please* ask them to wait until we're finished?"

Adam tried to appease her. "Well, Jasmine, they did claim this space first. Perhaps they should work for the first hour, and then they'll finish and be out of here." He lowered his voice and Hadleigh couldn't hear the rest of the conversation. Soon Jasmine stomped off to the dressing room in a huff, so whatever he said managed to reclaim the studio for them, at least temporarily. Vaslav shrugged and sauntered over to the side, where he began stretching.

Adam approached Hadleigh and Derek and said, apologetically, "Look, I know this is short notice, but would you mind rehearsing later in the afternoon in the future? She's kind of worked up right now, but she'll calm down."

Derek spoke up first. "It's okay with me, if Hadleigh doesn't care."

"It's fine by me." Hadleigh was more than happy to be at the studio when Jasmine wasn't around.

"Great." Adam turned away, visibly relieved.

The rest of the hour passed without incident, although Jasmine kept wandering in and out, pretending to tidy up the studio. When they finished, she followed Hadleigh into the dressing room.

"I hope you don't mind some constructive criticism," she offered.

Hadleigh bit her lip to keep from saying something she shouldn't, and Jasmine continued on.

"Giselle isn't a good choice for competition. Too slow. The judges want to see the bravura pieces. Frankly, Giselle just doesn't suit you. Maybe you two should make another choice." She pinned a stray lock of hair back, gazing at her reflection in the mirror. Then she smiled. "Just my opinion!" She waltzed out of the room.

Hadleigh wanted to break something. Preferably Jasmine's neck. She knew she was just up to her usual tricks, but it bothered her anyway, because she feared Jasmine might be speaking the truth for once. Maybe Giselle wasn't right for her. She needed to talk it over with Derek, and when she turned around, he materialized in the doorway, as if by magic.

"Hey, I couldn't help overhearing." He laughed. "Okay, so I was eavesdropping. I think that was the most complimentary thing she could have said to you, because if you looked bad, she wouldn't have anything to worry about. So it appears to me that she must be pretty worried—to try and tell you to change what you're doing! We must be looking goooooooood, dah-ling!"

Without waiting for her to respond, he swung his dance bag over his shoulder and said, "I'll see you tomorrow. Rest up! There's sure to be lots more Jasmine-sparring to come."

****

Hadleigh eased into the bathtub, as much to soothe her spirit as her body. Putting her feet under the running faucet as the tub filled provided a semi-jacuzzi treatment for her sore toes. But no sooner had she relaxed into the warm depth then the phone rang. Of course. Jann was out for the evening and Hadleigh was alone in the apartment. Debating only a second, she slid further down in the water and decided to let the answering machine take it. Her body was too sore to get up and relinquish the warmth of the bath. Just when she was about to submerge totally, she heard Doc's voice. "Hi, I hoped I would find you in by now. I'll try again some other time. I wanted to find out when I can expect to see you, but I guess I'll just have to call you later. Bye."

Hadleigh scrambled out of the tub, grabbed a towel, and dove for the phone. Just in time to hear the click at the other end. She slammed it back down, frustrated. *It was just going to be one of those days from beginning to end.* She left a trail of drips back to the tub.

Hadleigh had settled herself back into the warm bliss of the tub when she heard the rattling of a key in the lock and the door opening, announcing Jann's return. Hadleigh shouted from the bathroom, "I'm not getting out of here again for anyone or any reason, so there!"

"Wow. That's a fine way to greet your roommate. What happened to you today?"

"Trust me. You don't want to know."

"Hmmm. Let me guess. Does it begin with a 'J'?"

"You got it."

Jann noticed the red light on the answering machine and punched the button to play back the message. She listened for a moment, then said, "...and then I guess you missed his call on top of everything else, huh?" She chewed thoughtfully on her lower lip. "I think we need some *chocolate*."

Hadleigh groaned, then laughed. They both loved chocolate indulgences, and considering the day's events, she felt like she deserved some. "It's against my better judgment, but you talked me into it. I'll be out in a second."

"Don't hurry, I'll just run down to the corner and pick up some candy bars. Any requests?"

"Yes, something thick, chunky and decadent with lots of gooey caramel in it—but no nuts."

"I know, I know. Be back in a flash."

Later, when they sat munching and feeling mildly guilty, Hadleigh told Jann all the gory details of the day, including Jasmine's "constructive criticism."

"Well, of all the nerve! Of course, I don't know why anything she does surprises me. And," she said with authority, "you *will not* let her get to you. It's just what she wants. Pretend she doesn't exist. Or that she's covered with some horrible substance, or she has something green stuck in her teeth, or something. There. You now have my best psychological advice—for free." She yawned. "I am now going to bed, so all these chocolate calories can expand permanently on my hips. Goodnight!"

Hadleigh shuffled off to her own bed, but sleep proved to be elusive. She wondered how far Doc had traveled to make his call, and how long it might be before he would have a chance to call again. She would be sure to pick up the phone from now on, instead of using the modern woman's approach of letting the machine take it. She drifted off to sleep wondering what his life in the mountains must be like. What was he doing at this exact moment? Falling asleep under the same stars?

****

The performance season ended at last, but not the rehearsals for competition. Despite her hectic schedule, Hadleigh managed to negotiate a few days off, and soon found herself alone and somewhat bewildered in the Johnson City, Tennessee airport. It had been an uneventful flight, despite several plane changes, so she had expected to see Doc here waiting for her. But there was no sign of him, and, having no other option, she settled in to wait. It felt good and liberating to get away from the stress of rehearsals—and Jasmine. She now had a chance to read the historical novel she had started but never found time for in the past few weeks. It had been so long since she picked it up that she had to start from the beginning to re-familiarize herself with the characters.

She hadn't been reading long when she sensed him, even before she saw him. The air around her changed, and she felt the fine hairs on her arm stand up, as if responding to a static electrical charge. She looked up from her book, and there he was, rounding the corner with long steps and that efficient, animal-like quality he had in his stride. Her heart began to pound so loudly she was sure he could hear it all the way down the concourse.

He caught sight of her and his face lit up with a sincere from-the-heart smile that made Hadleigh happy she had come.

"I'm sorry I'm late. Sometimes it takes a while to get down off the mountain. As you will soon see." He slipped his arm around her back and pulled her into his embrace. "I am so glad you came. I was afraid you might decide against it, after all."

"No. There was never a chance of that." Hadleigh reached her arms up around his shoulders, allowing herself to be pulled into him. He kissed her gently on the lips, then said abruptly, "We'd better get going. Night comes quickly up here, and I don't want you walking up the mountain in the dark."

Hadleigh felt a pang of anxiety. But, she chided herself, she had to learn about his world and whether it was something she could handle— whether it was something she even wanted to handle. Smiling, she responded, "Don't worry about me. I'm a lot stronger than I look. I expect I could handle it, even after dark."

He looked down at her, his mouth easing into a smile. He hoped she could handle it, because he knew there would be more to it than she could imagine. He picked up her luggage, relieved to see it included only one large bag.

"I'm glad this is all you have," he said, lifting it without effort, "because it would be difficult to transport lots of luggage up to the Cove. I should have remembered to warn you about that."

"That's okay. Dancers travel light. The company doesn't allow us to carry much baggage when we travel. Most of that would be pointe shoes and other dance stuff, so coming here required *a lot* less."

"Well, if you forgot anything, or if you need anything while you're here, just let me know, and I'll try to accommodate." He slipped his arm around her again and they walked out into the fading afternoon light.

He hailed a taxi, and they set off. The city gave way to the beautiful, blue-hazed mountains that she had seen in the distance, and soon they were winding up and up on narrow two-lane roads. The landscape flashing by was stunning. A canopy of trees embraced them on all sides and from above, the ribbon of road winding its way through green tunnels punctuated with shafts of sunlight. Even the air seemed different. It was as though it contained more oxygen and was easier to breathe. Hadleigh felt almost a sensory overload as she looked around, trying to take it all in.

"How do you like it so far?" Doc whispered, knowing the answer.

Hadleigh smiled. "Wow."

They continued climbing, until at last the grade leveled off and they found themselves in a post-card-perfect valley, studded with small farmhouses and white churches, their steeples poking gently out of the trees toward the sky. It was so beautiful, it looked more like a Hollywood stage set than a real place, and Hadleigh said so.

Doc laughed—that deep hearty laugh that she had grown to love so much. "I hope you won't be too disappointed by the reality behind the set," he said, his laugh dying away, and his expression sobering. "The romantic Hollywood vision of mountain life is completely manufactured, I assure you."

They continued to spiral around more winding roads and were still climbing, always climbing. Suddenly Doc leaned forward. "Stop right here, please." He motioned to the driver, indicating a dirt pull-off next to some railroad tracks. He turned to Hadleigh. "I hope you're up to some walking, because this is where it all starts."

He hopped out of the cab, paid the driver, and slung Hadleigh's bag over his shoulder. With a broad sweep of his arm, he indicated the direction down the tracks. "Madame, this way please. It is only about three miles to the cove trail."

Then, suddenly serious, he put his hands on her shoulders and looked deep into her eyes.

"Please let me know if this becomes too much for you. I will understand."

Hadleigh stared at him, confused. "Do you mean

the walk—or something else?"

He hesitated. "Both." With that, he headed off down the tracks, Hadleigh falling in step beside him.

For the next hour, they talked little. Doc had lapsed into a silence that Hadleigh couldn't read. He seemed distant and almost agitated.

"Something is bothering you, Doc. Please tell me what's going on. Please."

Doc didn't slow his speed. "I'll tell you everything when we get there. Okay?"

"Okay." Second thoughts began forcing their way into her mind about this whole enterprise. He seemed so different all of a sudden. So quiet and far away. How much did she really know about him? Not much at all, she had to admit. Yet here she was, walking down a railroad track in the middle of nowhere with a sheer rock cliff on one side and a steep plunge to the river on the other. The water below looked rough and wild, with whitecaps dancing on the surface. She swallowed hard. For an instant she had the urge to turn around and run back. But she didn't—she couldn't. She wanted to be with him, near him, no matter what. She felt a compulsion greater than anything she had ever experienced before in her life. So she pushed her doubts away and kept pace with him.

"I gather this railroad isn't in use any more," she observed, determined to make light conversation.

Doc laughed, his expression brightening. "Oh it's used all right. But don't worry, you'll feel the train long before it gets here. You'll have plenty of time to step out of the way." He seemed to be relaxing a bit. He smiled at her. "Don't fret. I'll let you know."

No sooner had he finished speaking than he stopped walking. "There's one coming now. Just step over here under this rock, and we'll wait until it passes." He took her arm and led her off the track. Then Hadleigh heard it. A few seconds of low, deep rumbling, and then the train appeared.

Doc shielded her face with his arm, and they pressed their backs flat up against the cool rock. Hadleigh felt the rush of air, dirt, and coal chips as the freight train passed only a few feet away from them. It was exciting and more than a little scary. She stood still, protected by his arms, shivering slightly, until finally, it disappeared from sight.

"Wow. That was exciting. You do this all the time?" Hadleigh said, trying to catch her breath.

"Every day and twice on Sunday." He laughed again. "I'm only kidding. Normally I don't leave the Cove more than once a week, if that." He stepped back onto the track and began his steady pace again. He looked over at her. "But someone came along that changed that." He continued to stare at her and she blushed under his gaze. He grew quiet again.

They walked on, crossing a small railroad bridge, and beyond it the sheer granite wall began to evolve into a less rocky, more wooded landscape.

"We're almost there," Doc said, "and I want to stop a bit before we head up the hill. I need to tell you some things before we head in."

He turned right and began climbing up the steep hill. Hadleigh fell into step behind him. A few yards further and he stopped by a huge boulder covered with red and white graffiti. Doc patted the rock. "Have a seat. I'm sure you could use a breather for a few minutes."

"I don't really need one."

"That's okay. I'm not testing your endurance. I just want a chance to talk to you." He seated himself close beside her. "We are going to come to a rock cave here shortly, and when we go through the cave, I need you to hold onto my hand the whole time. Okay? No letting go, not even for a moment. It's important."

Hadleigh hesitated. "Okay. Sure. Why?"

"Hadleigh, you just have to trust me on this one. At least for now. I promise I will make all of this clear to you. But for right now I am asking for your complete trust. Please. I would never do anything to harm you." He took a deep breath and traced two fingers down along her cheek. "I will understand if you want to turn around and go back right now. If you decide that's what you want, I will see to it that you get safely home." He looked at her, a shadow of sorrow crossing his face. She looked back at him and squeezed his hand.

The road up the mountain was steep and rocky. It was more of a trail, really, with places where it became a labyrinth of exposed tree roots and rocks of various sizes. The path became harder and harder to distinguish as they climbed, and Hadleigh wondered how he knew where the trail was.

Doc led her upward, deeper into the woods, until they came upon the cave entrance. Covered by dense overgrowth, it was well hidden, and would have been almost impossible to find by anyone who hadn't been looking for it.

Taking her hand, Doc led her into the darkness. Hadleigh began to shiver.

"It's really cold in here," she said, nestling her body close to his. He put his arm around her, and she leaned into him, allowing his warmth to surround her.

"It's only a bit further, and then we will come out into the sunshine."

They rounded a tight, sharp curve, and Hadleigh felt a peculiar vibrational charge run through her body. All the hairs on her arm stood up again and she felt like the breath was being squeezed out of her lungs. Her skin tingled and she felt lightheaded. Afraid she was about to faint, she clung tighter to him. Then, as suddenly as it came on, the feeling was gone. They left the cold interior of the cave and emerged onto a beautiful grassy area that stretched out into the distance like a fine green carpet. There were apple trees visible, in full flower.

Beyond them, Hadleigh could see rooftops of small houses—cabins, really—tucked into the hillsides surrounding the area.

Doc stopped and studied her. "Are you okay?"

She smiled up at him, determined not to let him know how strange she felt in the cave. "Of course! It takes more than a cold cave to spook me." She changed the subject. "So this is your place! It's beautiful! No wonder you don't come to the city often. It's a perfect sanctuary."

"I'm glad you approve," he said without emotion, "but there is more to life here than the beauty. It is a hard and demanding life, as you will soon see."

They walked on into a small village that was little more than a cluster of houses. When they got to the center of town, children of all ages appeared out of nowhere, running toward them.

"Doc! Hey Doc!"

"Did you bring us anything from town?"

"When are classes going to start again?"

Then, seeing Hadleigh, they became quiet and shy.

"Hadleigh, these lovely young people are some of my students—and this one here," he ruffled the boy's hair, "is my nephew, Nathan."

"Pleased to meet you, ma'am," Nathan said, ducking his head and scuffing his bare feet along the ground.

"I am so pleased to meet you!" Hadleigh offered her hand and he shook it shyly. "I am happy to meet all of you."

"Okay now, go on about your business. I'll speak with everyone later." Doc hustled them off and led Hadleigh toward the porch of a small cabin. It was unpainted and scarred from years of exposure to the elements. There was a bench and rocking chair on the porch, and as they approached, an old dog rolled over lazily and yawned.

"Hello the house!" Doc called, pausing at the

bottom of the steps.

The door opened and out stepped an old woman, so wrinkled that her eyes were almost obliterated, but Hadleigh could still make out that they were the same riveting blue as Doc's. Her dress was faded and worn, but crisp and clean, right down to the snowy apron she wore over it.

"God bless you—it's Doc! Come on up! And bring your lady friend up here so I can get a good look at her." She opened her arms wide to him and hugged him long and unashamedly. Then she turned and did the same to Hadleigh.

"Welcome, child. I have already heard much about you. It is a pure joy to meet you at last. I hope you like our little corner of the world."

Hadleigh blushed, embarrassed at such an intimate welcome from someone she had never met. "I love it already. Your mountain is more beautiful than I imagined."

"Granny, this is Hadleigh. Hadleigh, this is my great-aunt Myrtle. She's raised just about every child in the cove in one way or another, and everyone calls her Granny."

"And you will too, child. I haven't answered to Myrtle since I was knee-high to a grasshopper. Even then, I didn't answer without putting some spit and vinegar in it!" She laughed heartily. "So come on in, put that bag down, and let me get us some cool apple cider." She led the way inside the cabin. "You'uns set right here, and I'll be right back." She disappeared into the next room.

Hadleigh studied the small space. It was dark, but her eyes gradually adjusted to it, and when they did, she became aware of more details. The room was sparsely furnished. There was only a faded sofa, a single chair and a table. That was it. A huge stone fireplace dominated one wall, and inside it an iron cook pot hung suspended over a low fire. Next to the front door a kerosene lamp perched precariously on a slanted shelf. Hadleigh looked up at Doc, who watched her expressions with a mixture of—what? Hope? Anxiety? She couldn't tell.

As if reading her thoughts, he whispered, "I told you it is a hard life here."

She nodded, beginning to comprehend. In a place this remote, of course there would be no electricity, no phone, and—she realized uncomfortably—probably no indoor plumbing. But she had done enough camping in childhood to know that it's simply a matter of adapting to one's environment. So, at least for the moment, she felt certain she could handle it.

Granny returned, balancing an overflowing tray. Tall glasses of sweetly scented apple cider were placed before them, and nestled under snowy napkins peeked sandwiches of thick ham tucked between slices of fragrant, homemade bread. Hadleigh took a deep breath. It smelled heavenly!

Doc dug in, and Hadleigh followed suit, the rumbling of her stomach making her realize how hungry she was after her travels. They ate in silence for a while, and watching them, Granny smiled, satisfied.

Soon the last rays of sunlight began to fade and long shadows deepened the darkness inside the cabin. Doc leaned back, stretched out his long legs, and sighed.

"I think it's time Hadleigh and I took a little tour of the place before we lose any more light." He put his arm around her. "How does that sound? Are you up for it after that trek up the mountain? It won't take long, I promise. Then I'll turn you over to Granny's care until tomorrow morning."

"I'm game." Hadleigh said, her apprehension spiking. She didn't want Doc to leave her, even for a moment. She never wanted him to leave her, but especially now, and in these strange surroundings. It hadn't occurred to her that he would not be staying under the same roof. But it was obvious Granny's cabin was intended to be her home for the night.

"You'uns go on, now. I'll get Hadleigh's room ready." Granny shushed them out the door, waving her apron. "Doc, you get her back here before dark now—you hear?"

Doc laughed. "Don't worry!"

They walked a few paces away from the house, and Doc put his arm around her shoulders. "I'd like to take you to the schoolhouse first, so you can see where I work. I've seen your place of ambition, now you can see mine."

"Sounds good to me." She fell into step beside him, and he pulled her close. Her body molded into his, their bodies nestling like two spoons in a drawer. It felt so right—sometimes—being here next to him. But then her pulse would begin racing. The surroundings and situation were so foreign. She felt doubts creeping into her thoughts like icy fingers. She shivered.

"Are you cold? I can run back to Granny's and get you a shawl. The temperature drops quickly up here."

"No, I'm fine. I do want see your school!"

"Okay, look up there." He pointed down a little worn path that wound through a grove of apple trees. "What do you think?"

The school building appeared as they walked under the trees. It was neatly whitewashed and even in the fading afternoon light Hadleigh could make out a small bell suspended in a cupola at the peak of the roof. It looked every bit like a stage set from Little House on the Prairie.

"Wow." Hadleigh wondered what Jann would say.

Doc led her up the steps and inside, where he stopped to light a kerosene lamp hanging just inside the door. He adjusted the flame, and the interior flickered into focus. Neat rows of desks faced the small chalkboard, and in the center of the room, squatting like some animal, was large black pot-bellied stove.

Doc swept his arm out. "This is it. This is where I hope to influence young minds. I have always known that I wanted to teach more than anything, and when the state offered me the chance to do it here, I jumped at it. Of course, I don't know how long we will continue to get funding. This location is so small and remote there is always a risk of closure. But I keep on, hoping for the best."

His face lit up as he walked around the room, talking about his students, the school, and what he hoped to accomplish. Hadleigh had never seen him so animated. He obviously loved his work—perhaps even more than she loved hers. She had always had such a love/hate relationship with the dance world.

He pulled two desks over near the stove. Hadleigh couldn't help thinking that it looked like a fat Buddha statue squatting in the center of the room. The thought made her smile. He glanced over at her, puzzled.

"Enough about me. Tell me what you are thinking so far. And oh..." Doc hesitated, clearing his throat. "I guess I should have mentioned that you would be staying the night with Granny. It wouldn't be fitting for you to stay at my place. That simply isn't done in the Cove." He cleared his throat again. "However innocent it might be. I hope you understand."

Hadleigh looked surprised. "I guess so." She had started shivering again.

Doc took off his jacket and placed it around her shoulders. "Oh, I noticed your expression when we talked about the night's accommodations." He fidgeted; easing himself into the small desk. "I'm afraid I'm just now beginning to realize that I haven't put as much thought into this as I should have." He reached out and stroked her face. "I'm not doing too well so far, am I?"

Hadleigh looked at him, then down at the floor. "It's just a lot to take in all at once. I knew you lived in a remote location, but why don't you have more...," she searched for the right words, "modern amenities?"

He dropped his hands away from her face, and he, too, stared down at the floor. Abruptly, he stood up. "I need to go and chop up some wood for this beast." He patted the cold stove. "It'll only take me a few minutes." He relaxed then and smiled down at her. "I have been lax in my duties here, and it's entirely your fault." He strode briskly out the door.

Chapter Seven

Hadleigh pulled his jacket closer around her. It was suffused his delicious scent, and she snuggled deeper into it. She could see him through the windows and watched admiringly as he raised the axe and brought it down hard, splitting the log neatly in two. He repeated the action over and over, working his way through the stack of wood. She looked at his defined, muscular back, and his arms—so strong—yet so gentle when he held her. She wanted nothing more at that moment than for him to hold her and never stop. Flushed with embarrassment, she forced her attention away from him and began studying the classroom.

The student desks were arranged in neat rows, and Doc's own desk, centered in front of the blackboard, faced them. It was a huge oak desk, fitting for a man his size. It was tidy and clear of papers, but with a stack of worn books off to one side. Her gaze wandered over the walls, covered with pictures drawn by the students. A forest scene, a house with pink smoke curling from the chimney, and a row of smaller works that looked like finger paintings.

Despite her best efforts, her focus drifted back outside. Doc had removed his shirt, and she felt her heart begin racing. He was beautiful—and she was used to seeing male dancers with gorgeous bodies. Yet there was something about him, some combination of strength and tenderness that she had never quite witnessed before. She forced her eyes away, fearing the sudden rush of emotions and trembling that welled up inside her.

Her attention came back to rest on the blackboard, where Doc had written all the previous week's assignments. It was all spelled out in detail—what chapters to read, and what papers were to be written. He had also included the date for the next exam: May 28, 1907. Hadleigh laughed. *I guess he must be feeling as distracted as I am lately.* But then, sometimes when she was tired she forgot and slipped into writing "19" instead of "20."

The hollow sound of his footsteps echoed on the steps and she turned around as Doc entered the room. He dropped to one knee in front of the stove, depositing the split pieces of wood on the floor. "Don't worry, I'll have it warm in here in just a second. I hope I didn't keep you waiting too long." The little black door creaked a bit when he opened it and began feeding the wood in. Soon the fire roared to life, and Hadleigh felt a rush of much needed warmth. She chided herself for not bringing her heavy winter coat. She hadn't expected to need it in North Carolina in the spring; and, she had to admit, she thought she was pretty tough after living through a few winters in New York. Well, lesson learned.

"I like your school, Doc. It looks like lots of good things happen here. I know you must be an incredible teacher."

"I like to think I make a difference. I spend most of my time—or did—," his eyes twinkled as he glanced at her, "planning lessons and activities. I want my students to be the best they can be. I want them to believe in themselves, and I want to feel that I have prepared them for the world as best I can."

Hadleigh nodded. "I know what you mean. I feel the same way when I teach little ones their first ballet classes. I want them to love the art like I do, despite all its warts. I hope to train them to be the best dancers they can be, even those who aren't the most gifted ones in the class."

Doc smiled at her, his admiration apparent. "I'd like to watch you teach sometime."

"I'd like to watch *you* teach sometime."

Doc laughed. "Well, that can be arranged. I'm supposed to start school up again tomorrow at nine." He pointed to the rope hanging near the front door. "I'll even let you ring the bell."

"It's a deal. Will you also let me write the correct date on the board?"

Doc stopped and the last piece of wood crashed to the floor. He hastily gathered it up, placed it in the stove, and closed the little door.

Hadleigh stared at him. Did he think she was criticizing his classroom? She hadn't meant any harm or disrespect.

"I'm sorry..." she stammered, "I didn't mean to criticize."

Doc shook his head and pulled the other desk closer to her. Without a word, he sat down and took both of her hands in his, rubbing their chill away. He looked at her intently for a minute, his eyes scanning her face.

"I guess the time has come, and I can't put it off any longer. I need to tell you everything—*everything*. Even if it means..."

He stopped, let go of her hands, and stood up, turning his back to her.

"Please hear me out. What I am about to tell you is going to sound unbelievable, but it is all true, every last bit of it. I find it hard to understand myself sometimes. It is why I brought you up here. You needed to be here—right here in this place— before I told you my story. So here goes." He turned back around and began pacing, running his hands through his hair.

"As I told you before, I am called Doc because of the mountain tradition of naming a seventh son. But I didn't tell you *why* we have that custom. A seventh son is supposed to be blessed—or some say cursed—with...," he hesitated, ""...certain abilities that are out of the normal range. For some it's the ability to see the future, predict the sex of an unborn child, or know when a death has occurred at another location. Things like that. We call it 'second sight.' But for me that wasn't the case. For a long time my family thought the tradition didn't hold true for me at all. That's because my gift is different, and I didn't discover it until I was ten years old." He came back and sat down beside her before continuing.

"I was out playing in the woods. My chores were done, and I was exploring, like all young boys do. That was when I first stumbled upon the cave I brought you through on our way up here. I thought it was the greatest thing in the world, and I was as happy as Christopher Columbus discovering America. So of course I had to go in and explore it. Well, needless to say, I was pretty disappointed when I found out that it just led back down to the old familiar trail up the mountain. So even though I wasn't supposed to go and play down by the railroad tracks, I went down anyway and waited to see a train go by. I was trying to salvage some excitement in the day, I guess."

Doc paused and glanced at Hadleigh, trying to judge her reaction so far. Her expression was unreadable, so he continued.

"I only had to wait a short while—you know what an active track it is—before the train appeared. Oh what a train! I had never seen one like it. It was huge—and *fast*! I had never seen any train go that fast up that steep grade. The trains I knew really struggled to pull up that hill. Also, this train had no stack billowing clouds of smoke. Nothing at all. I couldn't figure out how it worked. For days afterward I puzzled over it. So finally, even though I knew I would get in trouble for going down to the tracks, I told Granny what I had seen."

He stopped and adjusted the flame of the lamp higher.

"Granny listened to me without saying a word. She didn't even get upset with me about my going to the forbidden tracks. She listened and listened and listened. I can still see her rocking back and forth in her chair. Finally she stopped rocking and leaned forward. 'Doc,' she said, 'I believe you do have the gift. It's not what I expected, but I have heard tell of others with the same ability. Do you know what it is? Why do you think you saw a train that looked different? Did anything else around you look different? Think hard now—anything at all?'"

"I thought hard about it but I couldn't remember anything except the train. Then she said something amazing. *She told me to go back there and look around.* She told me to really study the area, and then come back and tell her what I learned."

Hadleigh shifted uncomfortably in the hard student chair. She wondered if he was really headed where she thought he was. *No, that's just my over-active imagination at work.*

Doc edged forward in his seat. He seemed to be just getting into his story.

"So I went back. Through the cave, down to the tracks. I looked around, and at first I didn't think there was anything out of the ordinary. Then it hit me! All the trees were different. They were bigger, *much* bigger. One in particular I remembered—my favorite dogwood—wasn't there at all. I ran back to tell Granny, but I think she already knew what I was going to say."

"When I told her, she just nodded and told me to sit still and listen. Do you know what she said, Hadleigh? Have you figured it out?" He stared at her, his gaze unflinching.

Hadleigh looked at the floor. She didn't want to say what she thought, and her stomach had started to churn. She began to feel physically ill. Doc's story—it had to be fiction—simply wasn't possible! If he believed it was—well...

"I don't know," she said in a choked whisper.

He took her by the shoulders, forcing her to look at him. "Yes, you do. I think you know exactly what I'm trying to say. And it *is* true. Oh, I know it sounds unbelievable, and I don't know how it works, although Granny has her own theories."

He stood up and lifted the lamp, holding it close to the chalkboard. "This date is absolutely true. You noticed it yourself. You *have* to know what it means. I wrote it down just last week when I taught my last class."

Hadleigh squinted at the writing, gripping the edge of the chair, her pulse racing. She shook her head. "No! What were you teaching, a history lesson?" She desperately began to make excuses for him. "You just forgot... you accidently wrote the wrong..."

Doc replaced the lamp and pulled her up out of the chair. He took her in his arms. "My beautiful Hadleigh—I know this is a shock for you. But I am *not* crazy, nor am I making this up. It is true. The current year is 1907. We crossed into it when we came through the cave. Do you remember feeling anything strange? I always got a sensation like a low grade vibration. You must have felt it, too."

She remembered how cold the cave was—and yes—there *were* those strange symptoms of lightheadedness, and the tingling of a low grade electrical current.

He continued to hold her close. His voice softened to a low murmur, and she felt the warmth of his breath on her neck. "That's why I ran away from you at first, and why I behaved so rudely when you first saw me in the restaurant. I didn't want to pull you into this. I was afraid—for you and for me. I am still afraid. Afraid you won't believe me, but more afraid that you will decide that this is more than any person can reasonably handle." He buried his face in her hair. "And I realize that I have come to care for you—more than you can imagine." Stunned and confused, Hadleigh didn't respond to his declaration. Instead, she just said, "Surely you don't really believe all this? You can't! Are you just trying to tease me?" She pushed him away, her eyes widening.

"It's not a question of belief. It's just the way it is."

He started to walk toward the door, his distant, cool manner returning. "I guess it's time to get you back to Granny's. You have a lot to think about tonight. I hope..." he paused, running his hand through his hair. "Well, I have to leave it up to you, Hadleigh. I brought you here so you would understand what my life involves. But I want you to know that no matter what, I will always love you, and always think of you, whether we are together or not. If you don't believe anything else, please know that. I will always, always, be with you."

He pulled her into his embrace and kissed away the tears that began to flow down her cheeks.

****

When Hadleigh awoke in the pre-dawn darkness, she wasn't sure where she was. She pulled the quilt up around her chin. The room was way beyond chilly—it was frigid. Shivering, she began to come to full awareness, and when her eyes adjusted, she was able to bring the little room into focus. She realized with a sickening jolt where she was. Granny had prepared the enclosed back porch as a makeshift bedroom for her. A small narrow bed, a washstand, and a straight back chair were all that could be squeezed into the space. But the bed was comfortable, and the quilt was soft and thick. However, with the door closed between her and the main room's fireplace, the temperature had dropped sharply.

She dug her way deeper under the covers, her mind racing back to the confusion of the night before. Sleep had not come easily, and Hadleigh tossed and turned for a long time, trying to sort out her jumbled thoughts. No matter how she looked at it, she couldn't make sense of any of it. It was impossible, so it had to be untrue. Despite Doc's sincerity—and apparently he believed everything he told her—her logical mind told her there *had* to be another explanation. Only one came to mind, and she didn't want to accept that, either. But she had to. As much as she loved him, she had to accept that he was delusional about this place. Maybe something had happened to him during childhood—a head injury perhaps—that caused him to have a false sense of reality. But he's teaching the *children* these falsehoods, and everyone is going along with it, as if under the spell of a charismatic preacher. With Doc's easy charm and magnetic personality, she could understand how people could be persuaded to believe in him. Even so, this whole thing was so far-fetched that they must be just following him blindly—like a cult.

Hadleigh sat bolt upright in bed. She had to get out of here! He had come a long way toward bewitching her, too, and she didn't want to wait around to give him any more chances. She was sure she could find her way back down the mountain, After all, there's only one way in and out, and as a child she had gone on many camping trips in the woods. She knew more than most about moving about in a wild setting, and once she got to the railroad, it would be really simple.

Her mind made up, she threw off the quilt, and, quiet but determined, she got out of bed, dressed, and collected her few things. Slinging her bag over her shoulder, she eased out the back door and into the misty dawn.

The ground was wet and cold, and the fog that

settled in during the night was thicker than Hadleigh anticipated. It hung heavy as smoke over everything, obscuring all but the outlines of trees and small buildings. She had to navigate by looking down at her feet in an attempt to stay on the narrow dirt road. Soon, that road faded into an overgrown, rough trail. She walked as fast as she dared, anxious to get down the mountain before anyone in the community woke up. She considered trying to find the cave again, since she had come that way, but she remembered Doc saying that the trail ended up in the same place. So she decided, mostly out of necessity, to stick to the path.

The trail was steep and littered with loose rocks of various sizes. Even with her dancer's training, she slipped more than once, but did manage to keep from falling. The fog didn't lessen as she descended, but she became more accustomed to it and increased her speed.

She continued, half running, half stumbling down the rocky trail, until at last, materializing out of the mist, she saw the familiar elephant-head rock. She slowed her pace, and feeling shaky and tired but reasonably safe, she collapsed on it and tried to calm her breathing.

The whole experience was surreal—aided no doubt by the heavy mist, and her lack of sleep. Hadleigh leaned forward, her hair falling across her face. She braced her hands on the rock and waited for her breathing and heartbeat to slow.

What a mess! How did I end up here—in this rural, desolate place, leaning on a graffiti-scarred rock in the middle of nowhere? She looked down and her heart rate jolted into high gear again. She brushed her hair back and blinked repeatedly, trying to clear her focus. She stared at the rock. Where was the graffiti? She ran her hands over the surface. Nothing. She jumped up and circled around the rock. It was clean. No marks at all. A sick feeling rose up from the pit of her stomach, and she took off again, running out onto the railroad tracks, and began to follow them back toward town.

She hadn't gone far when she felt the familiar vibration on the track. She stepped off, taking refuge under a rocky overhang and waited for the train to pass.

Hadleigh stood there, fidgeting and impatient, her back pressed up against the cliff. Why was it taking so long? It seemed an eternity before she finally saw it, pulling hard up the grade, belching smoke and steam. Her mouth dropped open in disbelief. She had never seen an engine like this before—except in pictures. It struggled to crest the hill, and then settled into a faster rhythm when it hit the more level area of the tracks in front of her.

Pressing her body against the cliff wall, Hadleigh watched the train pass. Had the whole world gone mad? Or was this nothing more than a bizarre extended dream? She prayed that it was. It had to be! Nothing else made sense. She slid down the face of the rock to a sitting position, and despite her best effort, her tears started flowing again. Never before had she felt so scared and alone.

****

Doc ran down the tracks, hoping to find her before she got too far away. He was relieved to see that she had made it safely down the mountain. He was well versed in reading the telltale tracks and signs on a trail, so he knew his worst fears had not been realized. Granny had awakened him early with the news that Hadleigh was gone, and he set off immediately. The woods were full of hazards, even for an experienced woodsman like himself—snakes being a particular threat—but especially so for someone as inexperienced as Hadleigh.

He made his way past the elephant rock and out onto the tracks. Far off in the distance, he saw her. A small bundle crumpled up against the rock face.

His heart almost stopped, and he broke into a run. Had she been hit by a train? If so, how could he ever hope to get her to modern medical care in time? *I should never have brought her here, the risks are simply too great.*

As he ran to her side, she looked up, jumped to her feet, and tried to flee down the tracks, away from him. But he was quicker and stronger. He grabbed her by the waist and pulled her into him.

She fought him, but he held her fast. "Hadleigh, stop! You don't understand! You must stop and listen to me!' He held her tighter. "Please! I was wrong to bring you here. I admit that. I just wanted it so much, I didn't think it through. You can go home! I won't try to stop you. I promise I'll make sure you get there safely."

Hadleigh stopped resisting and tried to calm herself.

He relaxed his grip and looked at her, his expression filled with anguish. "Hadleigh. My beautiful Hadleigh. You can't go home without my help," he said gently, "because I have to bring you through the portal—the cave. Don't ask me how it works, I have long ceased trying to figure it out. All I know is that I am the only one who can use the passage, and it transports me only into your particular time. No other. I don't know how, or why. But without me to bring you through the cave...well, *you can't get home."*

Hadleigh said nothing, she just stared at him. He released his hold on her and, instead, took her by the hand. He led her back to the elephant rock, and they both sat down.

"If you had continued walking down the track, do you know what you would have found?"

She shook her head, staring again at the inexplicably clean rock.

"I think you can imagine," he said, "since you must have seen at least one train. You would have found a town. A small town, and not the city you expected. A village, really, with dirt roads and wooden buildings. The few automobiles you might have seen would be right out of your history books, and..."

"Stop! I don't believe you!" Furious and stubborn she didn't care a bit if she was acting childish, until she looked into his eyes and saw anger—mixed with despair. Her voice shaking, she said, "Please...just take me home. I don't want to know any more. I don't want to see any more."

Then Doc's own stubbornness took hold. "No! I will take you home, but not yet." He put his hands on her shoulders. "Look, Hadleigh. Look at this rock. Where is the red paint? Where is the graffiti?" He wanted to force her to acknowledge the reality.

She shook her head, still obstinate. She didn't want to see. It was more than her logical, modern mind could accept.

He backed off, frustrated. "There is no graffiti." He said it matter-of-factly, then paused, trying to relax and let her take it all in. "There is no graffiti because *it hasn't been painted yet.* And it won't be. Not for many, many more years."

"No! It's not possible." She wriggled out from under his hands, shaking him off. "You can't really believe all this. It's not possible! The paint must have just washed off overnight—in the mist."

Doc sighed. "What about the train? Did you get a good look at it? Hadleigh—it was a steam engine. They don't use steam engines in your time, except as tourist attractions. They only have diesel engines. You can sit here all day, all week, and you won't ever see any diesel engines. Because they don't exist here—yet."

Hadleigh said nothing, she just kept shaking her head. "Please, just take me home—right away."

Doc rose to his feet, resigned. "I understand. I'll get you home right away. I am so sorry Hadleigh. I should never have brought you here. I was a fool to think that such a mad idea could really be worked out." Then, almost to himself he whispered, "But I was so sure you would trust me and believe me. Especially here, where you could see and experience everything for yourself."

He helped her up off the rock, gathered her things, and they began walking back up the mountain toward the cave. Hadleigh stopped and touched his arm. "I do believe that you believe." She said it mechanically, almost coldly, and that hurt him the most. He knew now she had convinced herself that he was delusional, and there was nothing he could do to change that. So he said nothing and they continued climbing. When they approached the entrance, he pulled her close to him, savoring her warmth, but she didn't lean into him like before. Instead, she pulled away, her muscles tense, not wanting to be enticed again. But he held tightly onto her, not wanting to let her go. He knew when he released her, it would be forever.

They walked through the darkness of the cave, and Hadleigh felt the same electrical sensation, the same dizziness and the same abrupt change when they emerged into the early morning sunshine on the other side. They headed back down the mountain, past the same rock, now covered with graffiti. *Was it really the same rock? How could it be?* Hadleigh looked away, not wanting to see, desperate to pretend none of this had happened. Her Doc, her wonderful, caring, handsome Doc, had suddenly become a madman. She was crushed, scared, and angry with herself. How had she allowed herself to become so bewitched? She had actually thought about giving up her career—her life—to make a new one with him. It had happened too fast. Way too fast. She had never felt so foolish. Well, she would never allow herself to be so easily swayed again.

Doc didn't say anything else, and they walked

the three miles down the tracks without speaking a word, the silence becoming a hard barricade between them.

****

The airport buzzed with its normal chaotic activity, but they managed to find a quiet corner. Hadleigh still wanted to run madly away from this whole situation, but despite everything, she still felt her heart breaking. Breaking because she had no choice. She couldn't stay. She had to forget him.

He read the confusion in her eyes and broke the silence. "I know I was a fool to try and make this work. It wasn't fair to you. I've had my whole life to come to terms with it, and it just seems normal to me. I guess I expected that since—I think—you love me, that it would be easy for you to accept. But I was wrong. I never doubted that you would believe me, and trust me, once I brought you here. I should have prepared you beforehand. Granny suggested as much, but I was too stubborn. I was so certain— positive, in fact—that you would believe me and just accept it. I know now that was asking too much. Too much for anyone. I just assumed..." he struggled, "well, I can see now how insane I must appear to you."

She nodded, still stubborn, still refusing to speak.

Doc got up and gently cradled her face in his hands. "I promise I won't ever bother you or make contact with you again. You don't have to worry about that."

She looked up at him, and despite her best efforts, the tears began to well up in her eyes again. Then the words rushed out. "I'm sorry Doc, I really am. But I *can't* believe you. You have to know that it's just not possible. It's not real." She started to pull away, then stopped. "I can't believe it—I can't believe you—I'm sorry."

He didn't protest. He just nodded, and she

turned to walk away. But his feelings overwhelmed him and he grabbed her arm and pulled her to him. For a moment she fell into the warmth of him, feeling the strong muscles of his chest against her body and the beating of his heart so close to hers, but abruptly she pulled back, pushing him away. "I have to go."

He dropped his arms to his side and backed up. "Hadleigh, I do understand. I just thought you loved me enough to trust me. Isn't that what love is—total trust in another person? I was so sure you would believe everything. I'll do anything else you need to make that happen. Just let me know what that is. Because right now I don't know what else to do, or what else to say." He stepped into her and caressed her face now wet with tears. "If this is what you want—truly—and the way it has to be, I will let you go. But I want you to remember this..." He paused to wipe the tears off her cheeks, "...I love you. I will always be thinking of you. So maybe I *am* crazy, but not in the way you think. Perhaps you will think of me, also, and in that small way we can share each other's lives. Whenever you are sad or in need, I hope you might find some strength in that bond."

Doc pulled her into him again, holding her in a firm embrace against his body, and this time she didn't resist. She fell into the urgency of his kiss willingly and wholeheartedly, savoring the delicious sensation of his lips against hers. Then, knowing her resolve was about to break, she pushed him away and ran down the concourse without looking back.

****

Hadleigh returned home feeling disjointed and confused. The weekend had already taken on the quality of a dream—or a nightmare. She threw herself into rehearsals with a vengeance, thankful to have an escape from her rolling thoughts. Jann didn't push her to reveal what had happened, but it was obvious something had. She knew that Hadleigh would tell her when she was good and ready. So she pushed her curiosity aside and resolved to wait until Hadleigh was ready to spill it.

But finally, Jann couldn't stand the suspense any longer. Late that night as they sat in front of the TV, she realized Hadleigh was just staring blankly at the screen, without a clue about what program was on.

"So, I met a great guy today at the morgue." Jann began with a smirk. "He's really good-looking, but he always smells funny."

"That's nice."

"He invited me out for a nice stiff drink. Get it?"

"Very funny. Where'd you say you were?"

Jann jumped up and stood in front of her, hands on her hips. "Hey! You're not watching TV, and you're not listening to me! You're not even on this planet. Snap out of it or spill it. I can't stand it any longer."

"I don't want to talk about it."

"That's pretty obvious," Jann said, her frustration level rising. Hadleigh usually shared everything. Eventually. So she changed tactics.

"What did he do to you?"

Hadleigh looked shocked. "Nothing! He wouldn't 'do anything' to me, as you so colorfully put it. He's not like that." She pulled the afghan off the back of the sofa and buried herself in it, trying to hide from the cross examination.

"Well? What then?" Jann yanked the afghan back. "You need to talk about it. It's eating you up inside." She paused and her tone softened. "It's just that I want my friend back."

Hadleigh's resolve weakened. "It's too unbelievable, and you'll think I'm crazy."

"I already think you're crazy, but that's what I like best about you. Most of the world thinks we're both crazy anyway for being starving artists." The twinkle came back into her eyes. "Well—almost starving."

"Hmmm..."

"Come on! Out with it."

With that, the flood gates opened, and Hadleigh described *almost* the whole experience. She left out the time travel part. She concentrated on the rural backwoods setting and details like the lack of indoor plumbing. Jann's eyes grew wider and wider, until she was rendered speechless. She was so stunned that when Hadleigh ran out of steam and stopped talking, all Jann could say was, "Wow."

"Well, I told you it was weird."

"Yeah. You sure didn't sugarcoat that part of it." Jann got up and walked into the kitchen. "I'm hungry. Do you want some chocolate or ice cream?"

"That's all you have to say? Besides, how can you possibly eat right now? I haven't had an appetite in days."

"I need food to energize my thought process, and eating wouldn't do you any harm, either." She disappeared around the corner. Hadleigh heard the suction of the freezer door opening, and Jann's muffled voice continued. "What'll it be? Mint chocolate chip or plain ol'chocolate?"

Silence greeted her, so she waved both containers in the doorway. "Pick now, or you'll get whatever I slap in your dish. And it won't be pretty."

"Okay, okay—plain chocolate."

"That's more like it." She rattled around in the kitchen for a minute then reappeared with two large bowls. Hadleigh groaned.

"Now I'll feel bad because I'm getting fat."

"I think you can risk it. You haven't eaten enough to stay alive lately, so I'm about to rectify the situation." She handed her a spoon. "Dig in!"

The ice cream did taste good, and Hadleigh knew she hadn't been eating much. She appreciated Jann's efforts on her behalf, and so, aided in part by the sugar in the ice cream, her mood began to improve and she vowed to pull herself out of the dumps.

"Thanks."

"Sure."

They ate in silence for a few minutes, but Hadleigh knew the wheels were turning in Jann's head. So she waited. Then, as expected, Jann mused, "Just where does he get the money he needs to travel all over the country to chase you? I'm sure a teacher's salary—especially in the backwoods—won't cover squat."

"Now you're acting like he's some kind of a criminal."

"No, I was just thinking hypothetically." She clinked her spoon down. "But really—it just seems odd that he would have sufficient funds to go traipsing all around the country—for any reason." She wrinkled up her forehead, then exclaimed, "Aha! You're right! All this can mean only one thing. He *is* up to something criminal!" The matter resolved, she picked up her spoon and finished off the ice cream. "Maybe..." she glanced over at Hadleigh, "...he robs banks or something."

"That's not funny!" Hadleigh laughed in spite of herself. The vision of Doc, his face hidden in a stocking mask and waving a gun, was almost impossible to imagine. But Jann did have a point she'd never thought about. How *did* Doc fund his journeys? He lived in such a remote location, with so few amenities—and well, if he had lots of money, wouldn't he use it to bring his family members down off that isolated mountain and into more—more—civilized accommodations? It was more of a mystery than ever.

Jann poked her with her spoon. "Okay, I've had enough exercise for my brain tonight. I'm going to bed."

"You go ahead. I'm just going to watch TV for awhile."

"Well, you're trading the experience for sleep, so try really watching it for a change." She got up, and Hadleigh heard her plunk her dish into the sink and shuffle off into her room.

Hadleigh stared at the flickering television. She knew she wouldn't have much luck sleeping tonight, between the sweet ice cream and her restless thoughts. She wanted so much to forget about Doc, but it seemed the harder she tried, the worse it got. She knew she had to block out those feelings, but it was the most difficult thing she had ever tried to do. Every time she closed her eyes, she saw him. She tried to think about the upcoming competition, her choreography—even Jasmine—to erase Doc's picture from her mind. But she had limited success.

She lay down on the couch, pulling the afghan up around her chin again. Without enthusiasm, she picked up the remote and began flipping channels. Nothing, nothing, and nothing. How can there be so much nothing on TV? She stared at the screen until exhaustion overtook her, the remote dropped to the floor, and she fell into a hard sleep.

Chapter Eight

Vaslav made his entrance into rehearsal with a flourish, like he always did, nodding at the accumulated dancers in the room before seating himself on the floor with his large bottle of Coke. He reached into his bag and pulled out a small bag of peanuts, ripped it open, and dropped them into his drink. Derek walked over to him. Vaslav smiled up at him. "Such nice things I get on airplane. I always get pretty stewardess to give me extra to save for later. They don't mind."

"Well, just don't get those nuts close to Hadleigh, she's highly allergic to them. Okay?"

"Allergic?"

"Yeah, we'd have to call 911 if she should eat or touch even a tiny piece of one. I'd been eating some once when I first partnered her, and her face got swollen and she broke out in hives. That was just from leaning her face against mine in White Swan pas de deux. So we all try to keep nuts far away from her. As a courtesy, you know."

"Oh, Okay! Sure! I won't let any get near her." He shrugged, wadded up the wrapper, and threw it in the wastebasket. "You not worry."

"Thanks." Derek walked back over to the barre next to Hadleigh, who was engrossed in stretching.

"Hey, I just did my good deed for the day. So you owe me a really big thank you. Really big."

Hadleigh took her leg down off the barre and feigned surprise. "Really? Shall I alert the media? What did you do? Tie my pointe shoes under the chair so I can't find them? Or perhaps you..."

"Very well, then. I won't be so generous again,

madam. You're on your own."

"Okay okay, I'll bite. What grand deed did you do for me? And how much is it going to cost?"

Derek lowered his voice and looked over toward Vaslav, now busily stretching his feet at the barre. "Be careful around Vaslav. He is always putting peanuts in his Coke. So if you have to shake his hand or anything, be warned! I told him about your allergy and that we were all careful."

Hadleigh touched his hand. "Thanks—I mean it! That was indeed a good deed." She smiled warmly at him.

Derek blushed. "Well, it wasn't *that* good a deed. I am merely protecting my own interest in this upcoming competition. I can't have you falling down dead on me right now. You'll simply have to wait until later." He winked at her. "So you see, it was purely self-serving. I am so ashamed." He rolled his eyes.

Hadleigh took a playful swat at him, just as Adam appeared and said, "Okay people, let's get started. Hadleigh and Derek, let's do a run-through of *Intensity* and see where the problems are."

****

The choreography took shape over the weeks that followed, and all too soon Hadleigh found herself on a plane headed for Jackson, Mississippi. She could hardly believe it! The International Ballet Competition! The granddaddy of them all, held every four years, like the Olympics, rotating between the U.S., Japan, Russia, and Bulgaria. She didn't think she had any real hope of winning a medal—this being her first year in contention—but the enticing possibility was there. The medals are awarded the same way as the Olympics: gold, silver, and bronze for the top three dancers. Hadleigh hoped that even if she didn't win, but placed high enough, it might provide excellent exposure for her, and help advance her career. She knew for the dancers who did win, it would be just like winning the Olympics, with all the requisite perks. A medal not only provides prestige, but also all but insures employment for the rest of their dancing lives. So although she didn't dare dream of winning a medal, it did occasionally cross her mind—what if?

At first, Hadleigh had been thankful that this was the year she wouldn't have to travel too far away from Doc, but now she wished differently. She wanted to get far, far away and immerse herself in an entirely different culture and experience. But it was not to be, and so she resolved to enjoy Jackson, Mississippi, anyway.

****

Hadleigh lay on the stage floor, staring up at the blind lights above. She tried to coax her rebelling muscles to stretch by pulling her legs, one at a time, over her head.

Sore as she was, she was ready. More than ready. She felt almost over-rehearsed and hoped she wouldn't make any stupid mistakes, especially on the easy parts. She knew that could happen easily if she got too comfortable in her role. Although she was more than ready to perform, Hadleigh dreaded the end of the competition. For the last few months, rehearsals had been constant and intense, leaving her little time to think of anything else, and thinking was precisely what she wanted to avoid. It was easier to forget Doc if she was too busy to feel anything except fatigue and sore muscles. She had hoped time would begin to ease her feelings of loss, but despite the passage of several months, the memory of him proved to be stronger than she expected. If she allowed her thoughts to go past her mental *No Trespassing* sign, her heart still burned with the familiar and unfading ache.

Derek appeared above her, smiling. "Are you warm enough to run through the á la second turns?" He paused. "I'd feel better if we did," he confessed.

"Sure." Hadleigh scrambled to her feet. The á la seconde turns made them both a bit nervous—it was a risky step. Revolving around on pointe with one leg extended to the side, parallel to the floor, she must complete one full revolution before Derek could step in and assist (or save) her execution. Adding a tutu makes it especially tricky, since it blocks his view of her supporting leg, and makes it difficult for him to save an imperfect turn.

They worked it through several times until Derek relaxed, satisfied.

"Okay, dah-lin'—thanks!" He slung his towel over his shoulder and sauntered off into the darkness of the wings.

Hadleigh practiced a few other tricky things from the coda, circling around the empty stage, then picked up her own leg warmers and walked off the stage to return to her dressing room.

Halfway up the stairs, Hadleigh met Jasmine. "What number did you get?" she sneered. "I got number one." She went on without pausing for a response. "I think that's an omen—a great one. I'll get to finish first and then just relax and watch everyone else." She punctuated this by looking Hadleigh critically up and down.

Hadleigh passed by without comment. Jasmine knew very well, and from the first day, that Hadleigh had drawn the last slot. The dancers drew numbers early on to determine the order of their performances. Most didn't want to go first, but going last, and having a long anxious wait, wasn't considered one of the better places, either. Hadleigh reminded herself that there was the philosophy that judges remember best what they have seen last, so if the performance is good it can work in the dancer's favor. At least, that's the hope she clung to right now. Besides, she knew all about Jasmine's not-so-subtle undermining tactics, and she was getting better about letting it roll off. She still wished Jann was here with her, sharing a dressing room, so they could laugh it off together. Instead, she was in a small room by herself. It was going to be a lonely wait.

The first round of the competition required the dancers to perform a selection from the classical repertoire, the second round a contemporary piece, and in the final section, choreography from both areas. Eliminations were made at the end of each round.

Hadleigh and Derek had chosen the pas de deux from *Esmeralda* for the opening round. Adam agreed with their choice and decided that starting with this piece would be a good way for them to get their feet wet. It was an exciting, character-style dance with a tambourine, and would provide a sharp contrast to the lyrical, slow romance of *Giselle*. It would also be a good venue for the judge's first impression of them. Now that Hadleigh had drawn the last slot, it became an especially good choice. If they should make it through all the eliminations to the final round, then *Giselle* would be a marker not only of their technical ability, but of their artistic talents as well. Adam hoped this would be a good strategy, since Hadleigh was known for her dramatic interpretations.

Hadleigh settled down in front of her dressing table and pulled a new pair of pointe shoes out of her bag to work on. She liked having something to do to keep hands busy, and sewing ribbons on her shoes served that purpose well. Plus, it insured that she was always a few pairs ahead when she needed some new ones, ready to wear.

She stitched in silence for a while, and soon the opening notes of Jasmine's music floated in over the intercom. Tempted as she was, Hadleigh refused to allow herself to go downstairs and stand in the wings to watch. She would know soon enough how successful the performance was, and the more distance between them, the better, anyway. It never paid to get in Jasmine's way, especially now, when everyone was under pressure. Hadleigh tried to concentrate on her sewing and not picture every step of Jasmine's choreography in her mind, but it was difficult.

Then, even before the final notes of the coda ended, the applause started. Huge, thunderous, and audible even through the backstage monitoring system. It was a pretty impressive response for the first piece on the program. Hadleigh dropped her needle and tried to steady her suddenly shaking fingers. *Well, I should have expected as much.* Jasmine was a dynamic, popular performer, and one who thrived on competition. She undoubtedly gave a flawless performance. Hadleigh sighed and tried to go back to her sewing, but her fingers weren't responding. Instead, she dropped the whole mess into her dance bag and decided to head downstairs and watch the other competitors. She walked to the door but hesitated, her hand poised over the knob. She wanted to give Jasmine enough time to return to her own dressing room, so she wouldn't have to bump into her and be forced to listen to her gloating. She waited until she heard her come bounding up the stairs and heard the door to her dressing area click shut. Then she slipped out of her own room and made her way down to the dark mustiness of the backstage area.

Hadleigh watched the other dancers from the wings for a while, trying to calm herself for her own performance. Everyone else looked good, so she couldn't really assess her own chances. *I guess I'll just go out there and give it my best shot and if it isn't enough—well—so be it.* She sat down on the floor and put on her pointe shoes, so her feet could get warmed up and accustomed to them. She knew some dancers who waited until just seconds before the curtain went up to slap on their shoes, but

Hadleigh always preferred to put hers on early to get a feel for them. She adjusted them now, tied the ribbons, and tucked in the ends in. She would go upstairs to her dressing table later and sew the ends in securely at the same time she put on her costume. She never wanted to concern herself about the ends coming out—or worse—coming completely undone during her performance. She'd have enough things to worry about once she got onstage, anyway. So, a few quick stitches provided her with the needed insurance and peace of mind.

She stood up and did a few quiet relevés, still keeping her eyes on the dancers on stage. Right now it was a young Russian couple performing the pas de deux from *Spartacus*. It had several spectacular lifts in it, and so far the muscular young man accomplished them well. His partner, thin and lovely, moved with abandon from one difficult sequence to the next. Hadleigh sighed and felt her confidence beginning to ebb away.

"They're no competition for you!" A voice whispered close to her ear.

"Derek!" Hadleigh had to smile. "You better not let anyone overhear you!"

"No chance of that. Everyone is too focused on their own problems right now." He paused and glanced around behind him. "You didn't see Jasmine's performance, did you?"

Hadleigh shook her head.

"I didn't think so. You big chicken. You should have. She did a good job, but it was pushed and too hard edge—for my taste anyway." He shrugged. "She didn't make any major blunders, and the audience certainly liked it, but I suspect the judges may not be that accommodating. At least I hope so, because then that opens the door for us! And we'll just walk on through!" He pranced around and swept his arm in front of Hadleigh like a footman with a carriage.

Hadleigh covered her mouth to stifle a giggle.

She could always depend on Derek to cut the tension.

"Come on. Let's go upstairs and relax for a bit. It's almost show time, folks!" Derek took her arm, and they pranced up the stairs together.

****

Hadleigh felt a rush of air slide past her as the curtain opened, and the heat of the lights warmed her skin as she stepped onstage. She moved automatically, her body honed for the well-rehearsed pas de deux from *Esmeralda*. Hadleigh knew the movements so well, it was almost as though someone else was doing the dancing. She and Derek moved like one person, transitioning easily from one section, one lift, one turn, to the next. Until finally, during the coda, the applause began to ring out, loud and long—drowning out the final notes of the music.

From the depths of the auditorium, screams of "Bravo" echoed throughout the house. Hadleigh stepped forward to take her bow and was amazed to see that the audience was standing! She smiled over at Derek, and he turned his head to hide a wink. She tried to relax, calm her breathing and take it all in. They had done it! No mistakes! No monumental blunders, as Derek loved to say. It was over! At least the first part—and now it was all in the hands of the judges.

The curtain shushed to a close, and they embraced each other. It was a great moment. All that hard work, and now the satisfaction of a performance well done. Adam ran in from the wings and hugged Hadleigh. "Great job!! You guys outdid yourselves!" He turned quickly away and walked toward the green room. He had to find Jasmine and talk to her, too, Hadleigh knew. She decided she wasn't going to hang around for that. So she slipped upstairs to her dressing room to gather her thoughts and her things and wind down from the day's stresses.

She dropped into her chair and uncoiled her hair. It cascaded down her back, and she shook her head to release it. She reached over, unscrewed the top of her water bottle and took a long, satisfying drink. Then she replaced the lid, set it aside and began to remove her make-up, beginning by pulling off her false eyelashes. Her breathing slowed but not her thoughts. She felt good about her performance, but not exhilarated—just relieved it was over. *I'm just tired. Tomorrow I'll get my energy back.* Then she remembered that tomorrow she'd find out if she did well enough to continue on in the competition, and she felt a quick jump in her heart. She took a deep breath. *Well, if I get cut, I get cut, and that's all there is to it. Then that's that and I can just go home and return to my normal life.* She stopped and stared at her refection in the brightly lit mirror. *My normal life.* It's been anything but normal—since—well, since Doc. She didn't want to go back to her old life, she wanted her life to change! She wanted to feel again the way she felt when she was with him. What she wanted was impossible. She put her head down on the dressing table and let all the pent up stress release itself in tears.

****

The next morning The List was posted. It was even thought of with capital letters. Those who would be going on to compete in the second round were listed. Those whose names were not on the list knew they had been eliminated. The non-posted then had two choices: they could return home, or they could stay, take classes, and watch the two final rounds of competition.

Hadleigh was spared the tension of looking, because she saw Derek flying down the steps even before she made it into the theater. She took one look at him and knew they had made the cut. He was almost flying.

"We made it dah-lin'!!" He scooped her up in his

120

arms and spun her around. "Isn't it grand?"

The theater door flew open and Adam appeared. "Okay, celebration's over." His tone was no-nonsense. "We need to start cleaning *Intensity*, and then concentrate on *Giselle*. I reserved a studio for ten-thirty today, and that should give us just enough time to get a short warm-up in before we get down to business."

"Okay, we'll be there!" Derek toned down his enthusiasm marginally but was unable to wipe the smile off his face. Hadleigh beamed in spite of herself. It did feel good to win.

****

He tried to stay away. But when the time drew near, Doc found himself doing something he never did—buying a plane ticket. He just had to see her again! He had to try one more time to convince her that he wasn't as mad as she believed. He not only needed to see her, he wanted to be there to give her some support and encouragement.

By the time the plane landed, however, his motivation had waned. He decided he didn't want her to know he had come—at least, not right away. He was afraid his presence might influence her performance, and he didn't want to be responsible for that. So he decided to stay in the shadows, as he had always done before, buying his tickets for the back row of the theater, where he could observe without being noticed.

The first night, he watched as Jasmine wowed the audience and worried that she would be the triumphant one. He didn't know why, but he didn't care for her performance at all. It seemed cold and forced. It didn't seem real or believable—at least to him. But he could see he was in the minority. The audience response was overwhelming positive, and they certainly knew more about ballet than he did. As far as the other competitors were concerned, Doc found them interesting to watch but not at all memorable. But when Hadleigh finally stepped onstage, he knew instinctively—even in his biased state—that her performance was something special. She seemed relaxed and natural. She moved from step to step effortlessly—or so it appeared—and her performance radiated a genuine love of what she was doing. When the last notes faded, and the lights dimmed, Doc found himself on his feet, yelling "Bravo" with everyone else.

He toyed briefly with the idea of going backstage, hoping that the surprise would be a good one for her, but he rejected that idea almost immediately. He didn't want her to know he was here. Not yet. So he gathered up his program and left the theater, walking briskly through the light rain that had begun to fall, heading back to his hotel.

****

It seemed to Hadleigh that between class and rehearsals and the accompanying exhaustion, the second round of competition flew by. It was as if time had been pushed to "fast forward." and suddenly she was onstage again, feeling the hot lights on her face, performing *Intensity*. The performance flowed by, the movements blending into each other smoothly and cleanly until reaching the dramatic fish dive at the end. The music ceased, and in the quiet, mesmerized audience, there was a pause of complete silence before the house erupted. The response was loud and long—much more than the previous night. Hadleigh and Derek took curtain call after curtain call. Then, just when the applause began to die down, she heard it. For a split second, and from far back in the theater a single voice rose above the others, yelling, "Bravo."

Hadleigh froze. She knew that voice all too well. It was Doc! Her heart pounded harder, as though trying to wrest itself from her chest. He must have followed her here! At first she felt that familiar thrill of knowing he was nearby, but then she remembered everything, and the thrill became a cold fear. He wasn't normal, she reminded herself. She needed to stay as far away from him as possible. He had promised he would leave her alone. But what if he wouldn't stay away? Was he now stalking her? Had she gotten herself into more than she bargained for? Her mind raced.

Derek pulled on her arm. "Come back to earth...earth to Hadleigh." He stared at her and noticed that the color had drained from her face. "What's wrong? We were great! Why do you look so scared? Oh, I know—fear of success!" He continued to pull her offstage. "Come on dah-lin', they're ready to clear the stage. I'm sure our public awaits!"

She stared at him, wondering if she should tell him what was going on so he could provide a safety net for her. He was a great guy, a wonderful partner, and a good friend, but she decided the whole thing was just too weird to confess to anyone, even Derek. Especially Derek. They knew each other so well from dancing together for so many years that sometimes he seemed to be able to read her thoughts.

"I'm okay, Derek. I was just a little distracted, that's all."

"I will accept that, but I don't believe it." He narrowed his eyes and became serious, a rarity for him. "Something is up with you, and has been for some time. I wish you'd let me in on it!" He stared at her, giving her time to cave and spill everything, but she said nothing. He sighed, realizing that she would never confide in him until she was good and ready. So he changed his approach. "Well, I'm going to get out of this make-up and go celebrate! Are you coming? I need my great and wonderful partner with me, or it won't be much of a celebration!" An inviting grin spread across his face, and his eyes twinkled. Derek could always make Hadleigh smile and forget her problems, at least temporarily, and for that she was always grateful.

"Of course I'm coming!" She gathered herself together and pushed the fear aside. Together they walked off toward the dressing rooms.

****

Hadleigh made her way through the long shadows on the empty stage, all the way down to center front. She had arrived early. She stood there, looking out over the vacant expanse of seats, and sighed. She had, as everyone expected, made it to the final round. She should be ecstatically happy, but instead she felt odd and empty—and odder still—calm. Too calm. This was the highest pressure night for the competitors. The margin of difference between the dancers at this point was small, and winning often came down to something as simple as making the fewest mistakes. But right now Hadleigh just felt numb.

She lay down on the stage floor, stretching her legs and staring at the rows of gelled lights overhead. She hadn't seen or heard anything from Doc, so she tried to convince herself that it must have been her overactive imagination last night. It was a highly emotional situation, after all, and she had probably heard someone who just sounded a lot like Doc. Or was it wishful thinking? She squashed that idea almost as soon as it crossed her mind. She stretched her other leg over her head and continued to stare upward at the colored gels. She thought about how much of her time seemed to be spent staring at, or into, colored lights. What a strange existence this is, she mused. It's not glamorous at all, at least not in the way she had imagined during her teenage years. It was more like a lot of hard physical labor.

The sound of approaching footsteps caused Hadleigh to turn her head, and the unmistakable shadow of Jasmine loomed from the wings.

"Oops! I'm sooo sorry! I didn't know you were

here. I didn't think anyone else would be in this early." She put her finger to her lips. "Shhh...I'll just go over in the corner and be as quiet as a mouse." She clomped across the stage and dropped her pointe shoes with a thud in the upstage corner.

Hadleigh groaned inwardly and rolled over. "It's okay, I was just leaving anyway."

"Oh, don't go away on my account..."

Hadleigh waved her off, gathered her things, and walked back upstairs, collapsing into her chair and staring blankly at her reflection. *I must be really numb. Even Jasmine isn't irritating me. Well, not much, anyway.*

As expected, Jasmine had also made it to the finals, so the rivalry, at least on Jasmine's part, had increased tenfold. Jasmine hated—really hated—to lose, and she had no intention of doing so, no matter what it took. Hadleigh knew it was best to keep her distance, and the greater the distance, the better.

Hadleigh deposited her pointe shoes on her dressing table and began to apply her stage make-up. It was still early, and since she didn't go on until well after intermission, it gave her something to do to pass the time.

She started with "pancake"—that age-old skin tone base that provides a matte, non-shiny palette for the make-up that follows. The performer's canvas, it prevents the dancer's face from being reflective under lights, and is so named because it comes in a flat, round container. Hadleigh unscrewed the lid, rubbed her moistened sponge across the light beige contents, and applied it to her face.

To kill time, Hadleigh put it on slowly and meticulously, one precise stroke at a time. She followed it with the shading, rouge, shadow, eyeliner and false eyelashes, creating those larger-than-life Disney World eyes. She managed to drag out this ritual for at least a half hour, but when she couldn't find anything else to tweak, she glanced at the clock and groaned. The pre-performance warm-up wasn't scheduled to start for another fifteen minutes. Hadleigh knew the hours before a performance drag on like the days before Christmas to a five-year-old, but tonight it seemed unbearable.

Once again, she picked up her pointe shoes and started to head back down to the stage. It was close enough to warm-up now that there would be enough other dancers around to provide a buffer between her and Jasmine. But before she reached the door, a voice on the intercom interrupted her. "Hadleigh Brent, please report to the green room."

Her heart dropped. Being paged this close to curtain time couldn't be good news. Dropping her shoes, she raced down the stairs two at a time, arriving breathless, just in time to hear Derek's familiar laugh. He turned and handed her a box.

"Looks like something interesting, for sure." He thrust it impatiently toward Hadleigh. "Open it! I can't handle this much suspense so close to curtain!"

She took the box and ripped into it. She knew immediately what she would find, and there it was. A small bottle of milk. She rustled through the papers, looking for a note, but found nothing.

Derek looked disappointed. "You have some bizarre well-wishers, dah-lin'." Shrugging, he walked away.

If he only knew how bizarre!

No note? Why? So it *was* Doc she heard last night, and obviously he was still here and planning to see the performance. Her heart began racing. How she longed to see him—feel him—again!

No! Hadleigh steeled herself. *I can't do this. I can't allow him to tempt me. He is delusional. He is not normal. I can't let him pull me under. And more importantly, I cannot allow him to distract me.* Anger welled up in her. How dare he! How dare he come back now, after promising he wouldn't—and appear during the most pressure-packed moment of her life!

She slammed the milk, packing and all, into the trash and ran back upstairs. Distracted now anyway, she grabbed her towel and water bottle, and, with a final glance at her reflection, turned back around and headed for the stage.

Reaching the semi-darkness of the wings, she paused and checked to see if Jasmine had staked out her place at the barre. Sure enough, there she was, center front, with her various personal items scattered around, punctuating the space as her personal property. *Well, good. Now I know where she's going to be, so there won't be any surprises—or confrontations.* Hadleigh leaned over and set her own things down, pushing them far back into and up against the leg of the wing so no one would step on them. She then walked deliberately to the corner of the stage furthest from Jasmine and began warming up, preparing her body and her mind for the performance to come.

****

The curtain opened to a blue-lit world and the mystical scene from the second act of *Giselle*. The audience quieted, and clouds of mist filtered across the stage. *Giselle*. The ballet was beautiful and poignant, and seldom seen in a competition. But Adam hoped it would be the best choice for Hadleigh and Derek because of their special combination of artistic and technical abilities. The hardest part for Hadleigh was her solo in the opening section. It was particularly challenging because it required exquisite balance and control, especially difficult to do in the semi-darkness.

She again felt the welcoming warmth of the lights on her skin, and heard the haunting opening notes of the violin and oboe. She allowed the music to wash over her—envelope her. She willed herself to merge into the character of Giselle and tried to shed her own personality so she could become, truly become, the spirit being. With those sounds and images filling her mind, she began the adagio. The audience hushed to complete silence.

Hadleigh moved effortlessly through the opening with its slow promenades and long penchée. No mistakes so far, not even a small wrinkle. She began to relax more into the role. Derek entered, came to her, and they began the poignant, yearning pas de deux of two lovers destined never to be together. They moved through the choreography smoothly, until many in the audience found themselves blinking tears away. Finally, the soft bells in the music sounded, and Hadleigh faded into the wings, leaving Derek alone on stage, reaching futilely upward. The lights faded to black.

There was a long silent pause, then abruptly the audience stood, as if of one mind. Waves of deafening applause filled the theater. The lights came up, and Hadleigh and Derek appeared together on stage to accept the appreciation, loud bravos sounding from throughout the house. It was long, thunderous, and overwhelming.

Doc knew at that moment she had won. Jasmine would be a distant second at best. Even to his untrained eye, he could sense that she had done something extraordinary. He also realized, and knew clearly at that instant, that he shouldn't—couldn't—try to coax her away from it. Even if she chose to leave this life for him, he'd always be afraid she'd regret her decision and come to hate him for it. He couldn't live with that. Doc watched as Hadleigh and Derek took bow after bow, the audience never seeming to tire. With that, he made up his mind. He would leave right now and get out before the crowd. He didn't want to see any more. He didn't want to be here anymore. It hurt too much. He needed to go home, back where he belonged, and leave her to a life that she obviously loved and to the many people who would see her future performances and love her, too. He knew now, with a stinging clarity, that a life with her was never meant to be. There were too many obstacles. Only in fairy tales did love conquer all.

He stepped into the aisle and bumped soundly into a slight woman who was sprinting in the opposite direction—toward the backstage entrance.

"Excuse me! I am so sorry. I didn't see you!" Doc backed up, embarrassed.

She looked up at him. "It's okay. I was just trying to beat the masses that will be heading backstage." She smiled, and added proudly, "You see, Hadleigh Brent is my niece! I flew in today to surprise her." She inclined her head, her expression puzzled. "Have we met before? You look so familiar."

"I don't think so." He hesitated, then said, "Congratulations on your niece's success—you must be very proud."

"I am, thank you!" She smiled and disappeared quickly down the outside aisle.

****

Backstage in the green room, Hadleigh and Derek were surrounded. The other dancers hugged and congratulated them. Suddenly through the crowd, Hadleigh looked up and saw Aunt Pat trying to get near her. She cried out in delight and pushed her way through the throng and into her arms.

"Why didn't you tell me you were coming? How were you able to leave the studio to be here?" She laughed, the relief of having it all behind her beginning to sink in.

"Slow down! I didn't want you to know I was here because I was afraid it might influence your performance. Better to leave it as a surprise for the end. And to answer your question, I *have* been known to leave the studio on important occasions!"

Hadleigh hugged her long and hard. It was so good to have her here. They hadn't been in touch as much as she would have liked lately, since her schedule had been so hectic. She resolved right then to prevent that from happening in the future.

"Well, shall we go out and celebrate? Or do you already have plans?" Pat asked, looking calmly around the green room at all the commotion.

Hadleigh glanced around, too. She half expected to see Doc materialize, quietly and mysteriously like he always did, seeming to appear out of nowhere. But she didn't see any sign of him, so she turned back to Pat.

"Let's go somewhere, anywhere! Just the two of us. I've had enough excitement for one night, and I want to catch up on everything. I know a nice quiet place. I noticed it yesterday when I was out walking."

Derek appeared, edging his way through the crowded room.

"There she is! The Great Hadleigh. You'd better get dressed—we're all meeting at Nick's restaurant for a big celebration!" He pushed her gently toward the dressing rooms. "And don't you *dare* tell me you're not coming!" He eyed her suspiciously. "Any and all of your guests are welcome," he added, grinning at Pat. "As well as any other admirers that might appear," he added, tweaking an imaginary mustache.

"Well..." Hadleigh began, but Pat cut her off.

"It sounds like a great idea. I'd like to get to know some of your colleagues." She smiled at Derek. "Your performance tonight was stunning, also. I'm so happy Hadleigh had you for her partner."

Derek blushed. "Thank you. I already know you must be the famous 'Aunt Pat' that I've heard so much about." He nudged Hadleigh and winked at Pat. "Don't worry, all of it was good."

Hadleigh gave his arm a playful swat. "I'm sorry, I am forgetting myself. Aunt Pat, this is my partner, Derek. Derek, Aunt Pat."

Derek, laughing, gave an exaggerated bow. "Pleased to make your acquaintance, ma'am. Your niece is totally incorrigible, but I struggled valiantly and somehow succeeded in whipping her into reasonably presentable shape."

Pat's eyes twinkled, and she turned to Hadleigh. "Is he always like this? However did you manage to get serious enough for your rehearsals?"

"Oh, he cleans up well," Hadleigh said, dashing up the stairs before he could take a swipe at her.

Chapter Nine

Alone in her dressing room, Hadleigh dropped into her chair and peeled off her false eyelashes. She hurried to remove all her stage make-up and get herself presentable for the evening's festivities. In just a few short hours everything had become totally surreal. She was so excited that Aunt Pat had flown in the surprise her! It was almost enough to ensure a completely perfect night of celebration. Almost. She pushed the thoughts that came into her head away, but they were resistant. She knew he must have been in the audience tonight, although she hadn't spotted him in the throng of well-wishers who had come backstage. He must have left and gone back to his hotel. Or perhaps he was waiting for her outside? She shivered and reached over to take a long drink from her water bottle. She hadn't realized how thirsty she had become. Normally she tried to hydrate herself prior to stepping onstage, but tonight the distraction of the milk package interrupted her routine. The cool water tasted wonderful and she took long swallows. But all of a sudden she felt the familiar, terrifying sensation of burning. She clutched at her throat, her heart pounding and her breath coming in short wheezing bursts. She felt that peculiar, heavy sense of impending doom. What was happening? She hadn't eaten a thing—only had a drink from her own water bottle. This couldn't be happening! But it was! Her vision faded in and out, and she rummaged frantically through her bag, trying to find the Epi-pen that would buy her enough time to get to an emergency room. But her fingers wouldn't respond.

It was already too late. The lack of oxygen, coupled with the exertion of the performance, overwhelmed her system. She lost consciousness, falling from her chair into a crumpled heap of white tulle.

A knock on the door sounded and Pat's voice called, "It's me, Hadleigh! I thought you might like some company while you get ready for the party. Hadleigh? Are you there?" She opened the door a crack and gasped, realizing right away what must have happened. She tore out her cell phone and called 911 while simultaneously digging through Hadleigh's bag in search of the Epi-pen. Grabbing it at last, she injected Hadleigh and prayed.

****

Doc walked slowly back to his hotel. He always preferred walking because it gave him time to think. Compared to the mountain miles he was used to, these flat city blocks were a piece of cake. He averted his eyes and stared at the ground as he walked, the bright lights of the city an affront to him, pushing back the night in an unnatural way, obscuring the stars he was so used to seeing at home. But mostly, his mind was on her, and only her, no matter how hard he tried to think of something, *anything,* else. He had so desperately wanted to see her again, to try and make her understand...and now, after her triumph, to share in her excitement of the evening. He thought he'd finally found an answer to how they could make a life together work. He had studied on it, and come up with a plan he was sure could work for both of them. Of course first he'd have to convince her that he wasn't a delusional madman. Ah yes. *That* was the sticking point. If he could just find a way to make her believe him and trust him...But he hadn't been able to figure that part out, and it seemed an increasingly impossible task. So he walked away—quite literally. He knew a clean break was the only way he could begin to get her out of his system, and take up his old life again. He had to start somewhere, and this was as good a time and place as any.

An ambulance raced by him, its siren screaming. He glanced up and said a silent prayer for the occupants. He always did that whenever he saw one of them rushing by with their fragile cargo.

****

Hadleigh awoke, the acrid aroma of strong disinfectant assaulting her nostrils. She blinked hard, trying to clear her focus. She realized with an uncomfortable start that she didn't know where she was. Wherever it was, it was awfully cold. For an instant she thought she was back in the Cove, on the sleeping porch of Granny's cabin. She pulled the covers up closer to her face, and the IV caught on the sheet. That's when it all came back. She'd had an allergic reaction, and she couldn't remember if she had ever managed to get to her Epi-pen. Yet somehow she had gotten to a hospital. She said a silent prayer of thanks and looked around for the buzzer to summon the nurse.

"Well, I see you've come back to join us, finally."

The strain in Pat's voice wasn't hidden by her attempt at levity, and Hadleigh mustered up a weak smile.

"I guess I got myself in trouble again. But I still don't know how. I know I didn't eat anything." She wrinkled her brow and changed the subject. "How did I get here?"

Pat reached over and smoothed Hadleigh's hair back off her face. "I found you on the floor and called 911. Simple as that." She smiled, relaxing a bit now that the crisis was over. "You really didn't need to go to such an extreme to get into the true character of Giselle. You were quite believable without the extra drama."

Hadleigh laughed and tried to sit up. "When can I get out of here?"

"I guess you must be feeling better, Miss

Independence." Pat studied her. "Okay, I'll see if I can arrange a discharge." She disappeared out the door.

Hadleigh pushed herself into a full sitting position and waited for her head to clear. She ran the events of the evening over and over in her mind. She knew she hadn't eaten any nuts, or been around anyone else that had been eating nuts, at any time before the concert. She'd even been too busy and distracted to drink water before the performance. But that's when the symptoms occurred—when she *did* drink some water, *after* the performance.

A cold chill, not from the room this time, crept into her body. Could the water bottle have come into contact with some nuts? How? Lots of dancers snack on nuts, but since it's forbidden by contract to eat or drink anything once in costume, it seemed unlikely that there would have been any food at all on or near the stage where she had stationed her bottle. So how had it happened?

A horrible idea worried itself into her mind. Was it deliberate? Did someone want her sickened so she couldn't perform? Hers was a competitive business, but she never thought anyone would be so cruel. Almost everyone knew of her allergy, since she had to mention it anytime she ate out in a restaurant or at a post-performance reception. Anyone at all could have tampered with her water. She often left it unattended, either in the wings or in her dressing room; either by itself, or tucked carefully into the side pocket of her dance bag.

But which competitors would be so—so—*criminal?* Most of them she hardly knew, and many of them didn't even speak English, or didn't speak it well. The scenario she didn't want to acknowledge kept surfacing. It had to be someone who knew her well enough to know of her allergy, and how severe it was. That meant it was most likely someone in her own company. The answer seemed obvious.

Jasmine? She could be a nasty schemer, but Hadleigh had never known her to do anything outside of verbal undermining. Though she was masterful at that, surely she wasn't capable of anything like this—was she? Even if she was, how would anyone ever know the truth? Peanuts are hardly a controlled substance. They could probably be found in eight out of every ten dancer's bags. If Jasmine had indeed contaminated Hadleigh's water, it was likely no one would ever know.

Pat appeared in the doorway, followed by a nurse. "It's official, you've been sprung! Let's get you dressed and back to your hotel. You have lots of people worried about you." The nurse busied herself removing Hadleigh's IV. Pat paced a bit around the room. She handed Hadleigh her clothes before she cleared her throat and said, "Hadleigh, I need to tell you that you have achieved front page news status here today. So there will probably be some members of the press downstairs that want to get a sound bite from you. Are you feeling up to it?"

Hadleigh's eyes widened. "No kidding? It can't be that big a deal."

Pat tried, but couldn't suppress a huge smile. "I didn't want to tell you right away, but my dear, when you're a gold medalist in an international competition, that alone is newsworthy—albeit probably buried on the back page. But now you can imagine the stir your—umm—incident has created. It has catapulted you into front page status."

Hadleigh sat bolt upright, pulled her gown off, and tugged her shirt on over her head, the news taking a moment to comprehend. "I won? Really?" Then, unable to contain her excitement, she hopped off the bed, hugging Pat hard.

"Calm down, young lady, or I'll have to pretend you're eight years old again!" She pushed her gently back down into a sitting position. "You need to take it easy for a bit. You had a close call," she added in a stern tone of voice.

Hadleigh nodded, marginally toning down her enthusiasm. "Where's Derek? I need to talk to him. He must be beside himself and completely out of control by now. I need to be around to rein him in."

"You can call him when we get back to the hotel—if he isn't already there waiting for you, as I expect. So let's get moving."

Magically, another nurse appeared in the doorway. "Hello Miss Brent. I'm from Transportation." She pushed a wheelchair into the room.

Hadleigh looked at it and frowned. "Please—I don't need it. How embarrassing for a dancer to be taken out in a wheelchair when I feel perfectly okay."

"Sorry, hospital regulations." Her face was pleasant, but her tone was no-nonsense.

Hadleigh looked pleadingly at Pat, but she was unmoved.

"Come on, no one will doubt your dance ability if they see you taking advantage of such a special hospital service."

With a sigh, Hadleigh allowed herself to be wheeled downstairs to the lobby, but she wasn't prepared for the scene that awaited her outside. The front of the hospital was teeming with reporters and cameras.

Pat leaned over and whispered, "Just give them a short statement, and we can be on our way."

"What happened to you, Miss Brent?"

"Do you think it was a deliberate attempt on your life?"

"How are you feeling now?"

"How does it feel to win under these circumstances?"

The questions assaulted her from all sides, microphones thrust into her face.

Hadleigh swallowed hard and said simply, "I'm

feeling fine now, and I just want to get back to my normal life. Thank you."

With that, Pat wheeled her outside to her waiting car, leaving the shouts of the crowd behind.

****

Hadleigh never saw him. There had been too many people in the throng that waited outside the hospital. Yet he was there, trying to jostle his way to the front to get near her. But she was whisked away too quickly, and in a flash she was nothing more than two red taillights winking off in the distance.

The previous night Doc arrived at his hotel room just in time to see and hear the breaking headlines: "American Gold Medal Winner Collapses." The limited details scrolled across the bottom of his screen, and he watched in horror. He abandoned all his plans and raced to the hospital, frustrated when he was denied admittance along with everyone else. Undeterred, he claimed a chair for himself in the lobby and waited, terrified. All night long he sat there, shifting uncomfortably, never even dozing off, and pestering the nurses by asking on the hour what her condition was. Even when it became clear the crisis was over, he continued to stay. He had to see for himself that she was really okay, and try to let her know he was there for her. He wanted desperately to take care of her, especially now, and to make everything all right again. When she appeared at last, looking even paler than she did in last night's white make-up of Giselle, he couldn't get anywhere close to her, the crush of other human bodies was too great.

Increasingly frustrated and out of options, he returned to his hotel to think. He hated all this city stuff more and more. The push of the people, the push of the buildings and the concrete that crowded out the green growing things he loved so much. He wanted more than ever to take her away from all this. Worst of all was what he kept hearing over and over on the television: that someone had done this to her *deliberately*. The idea was abhorrent to him. Indeed, he found it almost unbelievable. Someone had tried to hurt her, and could have killed her! Now he wasn't ready to walk away—not without taking her with him. Oh no! Now he was determined to do whatever he needed to do to prove to her that he wasn't mad, and that everything he told her, and showed her, was real. This time there would be no giving up and no walking away. He *had* to succeed. There was no other choice. And once she believed him, he could rescue her from all this madness, and she would be happy to go with him. For how could she want to live in a world that could do this to her?

****

Hadleigh could hardly believe it. The police were investigating the "incident," as the media called it to rule out "foul play." Hadleigh was certain she knew who was responsible—and equally sure there would be no way to prove it. Jasmine would have been smart about it. For all her faults, Jasmine wasn't stupid. Indeed, she was exceedingly clever and creative. But how she had managed to do it baffled Hadleigh, and she knew in her heart it would probably always remain a mystery.

The police had dusted "the scene" for prints and had taken all of Hadleigh's personal belongings from the theater, including the water bottle, on which they were running tests. But even if Jasmine's (or anyone else's) fingerprints were found, they would still have plausible deniability. Dancers share many of their items, and anyone could have simply picked up Hadleigh's bag to move it out of the way in the wings—or some other similar scenario, thus putting their prints on her bag or bottle. Therefore Hadleigh didn't have much hope of the police finding definitive evidence as to who spiked her drink. At this point, she was too tired and confused to care. What was done was done.

The big debate now circled around the medal ceremony. It had been scheduled for that evening, but had been postponed until a decision could be reached about whether to cancel it entirely. There was the obvious security issue: If it was held, would it be safe for Hadleigh to attend? The discussion raged behind closed doors for the better part of the day. Hadleigh and Pat waited anxiously in the hotel for the final word, Hadleigh trying to rest, and Pat pacing up and down.

The call finally came, and the news was good. The ceremony would proceed on schedule, albeit with added security. And, Hadleigh realized uncomfortably, probably lots of added media attention. She would be required to be accompanied by security personnel at all times, but she would be permitted to attend and receive her medal.

****

The ceremony came and went in a crush of cameras and reporters, but with a proud and relieved Aunt Pat sitting center front as Hadleigh had the gold medal placed around her neck. It was a wonderful moment after all, despite the intrusions. It was as though everything she'd ever dreamed of in her life had come true—although not without some pretty heavy and unexpected baggage. Yet, even as she reveled in the moment, she struggled inwardly, trying to understand her churning emotions. Although she was very *very* happy to have won, she wasn't feeling as ecstatic as she expected. Deep down, she knew her mixed feeling weren't due to the "incident" either. There had come to reside in her an emptiness that nothing seemed to fill, and although she didn't want to admit it, or think about it, she knew what the problem was, and why there was still an aching in her heart.

Her state of mind did not go unnoticed by Aunt Pat. After the ceremony, Hadleigh joined her in her hotel room for a private celebration and some well-deserved "down time." Pat had shelved the champagne and instead had purchased some sparkling grape juice. She poured it into two wine glasses and sat down beside Hadleigh.

"Are you going to tell me what else has been bothering you? I am pretty sure it's not just this most recent problem of the peanut incident." She took a long sip of juice. "We'll just have to wait for the findings of the investigation before we dwell on that. Right now, I want you to tell me what else is up, because it is pretty evident *something* is." Pat stared into her face. "You and I were always able to talk, so let me in on it."

Hadleigh ran her finger slowly around the base of her glass. "I don't really know. I *am* happy—very happy. I just..."

"Just what?"

Hadleigh hesitated, so Pat continued.

"I will confess that I spoke with Jann last night. She called to see how you were doing, and she filled me in on the rest of it."

"Oh." Hadleigh continued to stare into her glass. "What did she say?"

"Not much. She clearly didn't want to betray any confidences. But she said enough so I know it has to do with a certain gentleman."

Then there was no holding back. The tears overflowed, and Hadleigh revealed everything. Or, almost everything. She left out the most critical part. Pat listened to the whole story, and when Hadleigh finished, she said, matter-of-factly, "So what's wrong with him? Why have you decided not to see him anymore, since he obviously wants to see you, and I can tell you care about him?"

Hadleigh squirmed. How could she tell anyone, even her beloved Aunt Pat, such a bizarre story? She didn't want to make her worry any more than necessary about her life—especially after last night. She wanted her to be proud of her accomplishments and secure in the knowledge that she had raised her sister's child to be a competent adult.

"I don't know how...that is...it's too strange to be believed."

"Try me."

Hadleigh took a long swallow of juice. She desperately needed to confide in someone. "Okay."

Pat settled down next to her. "Go ahead."

The floodgates opened. Pent up for so long, it was a relief to finally let it out and tell someone. Hadleigh described everything—every detail—right down to the graffiti on the rock and the strange electrical sensation in the cave. She was so involved in her story she didn't notice when Pat got up and began to pace back and forth in front of the window. Her aunt was clearly disturbed.

Hadleigh stopped for a moment and moistened her lips. She shook her head. "I know this sounds completely crazy, and so that's why I can't see him anymore. There *is* something wrong with him! He is obviously delusional."

"Does Jann know all about this?" Pat paused, mid-step.

"No, I haven't told anyone—until now."

Pat began pacing again. She walked back and forth, rolling the napkin in her hand into a tight ball, then unrolling it again. Over and over. Finally she stopped and turned to Hadleigh. "I need to think about this for awhile. Let's both go to bed, and we'll talk again in the morning."

Hadleigh glanced at her, surprised. "Why?"

"Let's just say we both need a good night's rest and leave it at that," Pat said brusquely, ending the discussion. She walked Hadleigh to the door, kissing her on the cheek. "Sweet dreams and congratulations. You have handled a difficult situation with style and grace. I don't know anyone who could have done better."

Hadleigh hugged her long and hard before

turning away toward the elevators. But alone in her own room, she couldn't fall asleep. She was too wound up from the excitement and anxiety of the past days and Aunt Pat's strange reaction to her story about Doc. And what about Doc? Was he in attendance at the performance? If so, why didn't he come backstage, and if he had, was he there when the ambulance took her away? He sent her the milk, and he had no way of knowing she had thrown it out. Of course, even if he had come back, she wasn't sure how she would have reacted. He probably guessed that. Doc was pretty in tune with her feelings, all right. With that thought, Hadleigh rolled over, determined to will herself to sleep.

Sleep refused to come. She tossed for most of the night, her thoughts churning with so many questions, so many concerns. Why did Aunt Pat seem so disturbed? Did she think Hadleigh was losing her mind? Maybe she shouldn't have told her the whole story. But she had always shared everything with her, and their relationship had always been close. Was she afraid Hadleigh would continue to see Doc anyway, despite his strange beliefs? Would she forbid it? Hadleigh was all grown up, a legal adult, but she would still have a hard time going against Pat's wishes. *Wait a minute...I had already decided to leave him alone. What am I thinking?* Hadleigh rolled over and clicked on the TV just to have something to distract her jumbled thoughts. It wasn't until the early hours of the morning, with the TV flickering in the darkness, that she fell into a fitful sleep.

****

"Hadleigh, he may not be delusional."

Aunt Pat's pronouncement over breakfast blindsided Hadleigh.

She gasped. "How can that be?"

"I think I saw him last night in the theater. Actually, I quite literally ran into him. Did you know he was there?"

Hadleigh nodded. "I was pretty sure. He sent me a package backstage. But I...I threw it away." She bit her lip. "Wait! How did you know who it was?"

Pat took a deep breath. "I knew because I had seen him before—many years ago." She hesitated. "Almost before you were born."

"That's not possible. He's not old enough."

Pat sat down and put her arms around Hadleigh. "I need to tell you something. It never seemed terribly important, and yet it was something I was never able to forget. It all came back to me, vividly, the other night as I waited in the hospital corridor for word on how you were doing. It was so much like...another time, not so long ago. Anyway, well...I was awake most of the night trying to make sense of it. Then all of a sudden it became clear. Strangely, perfectly clear." She sighed. "I know it all sounds insane, but the pieces fit, and it answers a question I always wondered about."

Hadleigh's eyes widened. What secrets hadn't she been told? She knew from an early age that her mother had died in childbirth, and her father had died in a car accident when her mother was late into her pregnancy with her. That's how she came to be adopted by Aunt Pat, her mother's sister. Hadleigh had seen many pictures of her parents, and her background had never been a secret. So what other revelation could there be?

Pat took a sip of tea and a bite of muffin before she continued. Hadleigh fidgeted impatiently.

"On the day you were born, I was waiting around outside the nursery to catch my first glimpse of you; in a hospital hallway that looked and smelled just like the one I waited in the other night. But back then, it was all so exciting—but sad too, because your father wasn't there. At this time your sweet mother was doing fine, and we had no idea of the...the greater sadness...to come." She stopped and brushed the crumbs off her hands.

"Anyway, the corridor in front of the nursery was empty except for one very old man. I assumed he was the grandfather, or perhaps great-grandfather, of one of the other expected newborns. He was striking, even in his advanced years, and I suppose that's why I noticed him. He had the most riveting blue eyes, still alert and clear even at his age. Yet he seemed so sad—like life had dealt him some great hardships, and he just kept walking slowly back and forth in front of the nursery's observation glass."

"Who was he?" Hadleigh interrupted, her hands beginning to shake.

Pat stood up and began pacing in front of the window, like she had the night before. She ignored Hadleigh's question and continued. "When they brought you out—Oh! You were the most beautiful baby I had ever seen ..." Her eyes welled with tears, and she stopped and gazed out the window into the distance.

"You didn't even cry. You just looked around like you were fascinated by everything." She turned back to face Hadleigh. "Now I know every aunt thinks their niece is the most beautiful one in the world, but you *were*—truly!"

Hadleigh blushed. She had never heard this part of the story before. She only knew that things had turned tragic rapidly, with her mother hemorrhaging and the doctors being unable to save her. Pat began pacing again.

"Anyway, the old man continued to stare into the nursery window, and when I started to go back down the hall to your mother's room I noticed something odd. He was crying. He was crying and doing this peculiar movement. He kept squeezing his left hand into a fist—one, two, three times—then he'd pause and repeat it. All the while he kept staring at you and running two fingers down the glass—over and over again ..." She demonstrated on the hotel window. "It was so strange, yet so moving. All the while, he never stopped crying. It was as though his heart was breaking."

Hadleigh's heart pounded. She watched Pat's fingers trace two lines down the condensation on the glass. She knew what he had been doing. He always used two fingers to caress her face—never his whole hand. And well she knew the three squeezes.

Pat continued on. "When I walked past him and caught his eye, he looked almost afraid. Then he turned and walked in slow, small steps down the hall and out of sight. I never saw him again. But I always remembered him, and the strange way he ran his fingers down the glass."

"How did you know he was looking at me?" Hadleigh had to ask. "There must have been lots of babies in the nursery."

Pat sighed. "No, my dear. At that particular time, you were the only baby there. So there is no doubt who he was looking at."

"Did you ever try to find out who he was?" Hadleigh said, although she knew the answer. It did make sense—a crazy, mixed-up, unbelievable kind of sense.

"Yes, I asked a couple of the nurses, but no one had ever seen him before. And after your mother...well, the old man was quite forgotten, under the circumstances."

Hadleigh looked down at her half-eaten breakfast and tried to stop her hands from shaking.

After a long pause, she whispered, "It was Doc. I know it was."

Pat nodded and wrapped her arms around her. "I went over and over it in my mind last night. It seems too impossible, but it makes sense, doesn't it? Or at least, as much sense as something this unbelievable can make. The man who bumped into me after the performance—I knew he looked familiar, and last night I realized it had to be the same person."

****

The peanut incident investigation concluded much faster than anyone expected, because the culprit came forward voluntarily. It was Vaslav. He confessed he'd taken a few sips from Hadleigh's bottle after the warm-up. It was conveniently right there in the back of the wings; and he had been eating nuts before—up in his dressing room. So he admitted he must have been the one who contaminated her water. This was borne out by the forensics. His fingerprints were found on the bottle. So, case closed. He apologized profusely to Hadleigh and Pat, but Hadleigh didn't buy the story for one minute. She was certain it had been Jasmine's doing and she either did it alone or with Vaslav's help. What a perfect alibi! There was absolutely nothing to prove otherwise. But Hadleigh thought Jasmine didn't realize how serious the consequences of her little scheme could be. Surely she would never have intended to produce fatal results! At least Hadleigh refused to believe she would have been that much of a sociopath. She probably just wanted Hadleigh to become just sick enough to be out of the final round of competition, and thus open the door for her and Vaslav. Simple as that. Hadleigh desperately needed to believe that was all Jasmine intended, and that she had gotten a good, soul-shattering scare. Perhaps that would keep her on the straight and narrow from now on, especially since they had to go on working together in the same environment.

Hadleigh shuddered. She was not looking forward to going back to work under these circumstances. Jasmine had always been hard to tolerate—but now! She wasn't sure how she was going to handle the first confrontation with her, or how she was going to deal with the day to day situations that were sure to arise now that Hadleigh had beaten her in the competition. So it was with a heavy heart that Hadleigh left Jackson; and, she realized, it wasn't just because of Jasmine and the peanut incident.

What about Doc? Could it be that everything he told her was true? Aunt Pat seemed to think so, and the evidence spoke for itself. But then, so did the "evidence" of Vaslav and the water bottle. How dependable was such evidence, really? Was it truly Doc that Pat had seen so many years before? Or was it just someone who looked like him? But the two fingers—the three squeezes! It had to be Doc! It all had to be true. Hadleigh wanted it to be, desperately, passionately, but even if it was, where did that leave her? She had no way to contact him, and since he hadn't shown up to find her, he must have returned to the mountain—and his time. What could she do about it? Nothing. She could only wait and pray he would return to find her, like he'd always done before.

Chapter Ten

Granny said nothing, she just continued to rock. Doc paced up and down the steps, finally sitting down on the middle one, resting his elbows on his knees.

"I thought about showing her some of the furniture pieces I'd been selling in her time. You know, those nice old pieces from that hotel they tore down last year. It was stuff nobody else wanted...nobody around here, anyway." He rubbed his temples, "But they wouldn't look any different to her than something I could have purchased in an antique store in New York."

Granny kept silent, and all he could hear was the steady thrump thrump thrump of her rocker.

"Then I remembered the stamps. The dealer I work with in her time is always amazed at the mint condition stamps I bring in. But again, she's going to think I purchased them at some stamp auction just to try and convince her." He sighed, and shrugged. "I'm afraid I've run out of options."

The thrumping slowed to a stop, and Granny stared out over the mountains for a long time. Doc said nothing, knowing her well enough to wait. Finally, she pushed herself up out of the chair and walked over to the porch railing. She looked down at him.

"Well Doc. The way I see it, you aren't shy of options. Not completely. There is one left."

He turned his head toward her, hope flickering across his face. "What?"

"Trust." She said it simply and matter-of-factly, nodding her head with assurance.

The hope faded from his eyes, and he stared back at his shoes. "Oh."

She stared down at him, her mouth set in a firm line. "Now Doc, git up off of them steps and come up here in front of me, so's I can speak my mind plainly."

Doc rose, and in one long stride came to stand beside her. His large frame cast a long shadow over her. "Say your piece, Granny. I'm listening."

She placed her hand on his. "It's clear. The choice is no longer up to you. It's up to *her*. You have to believe that she loves you enough to trust you. Completely. She must trust what you tell her. Oh, I admit that it is a trust beyond reason, but..." she patted his hand, "...love without trust is just a big bunch of nothin', ain't it? It's certainly not something a body can build a life on."

Doc nodded slowly. "Of course, you're right." He clenched his jaw. "I need to get on with my life and put all this behind me."

"Now Doc, I didn't say that. I'm just saying there's only one thing you can do—right in the here and now." She took her hand away and stood with her hands on her hips, studying him. Then she smiled. "Doc, something brought you two together—against all odds. So..." she hesitated, "...maybe it's meant to be. Maybe it ain't. But there *is* one thing you can do, and need to do, no matter what. I think, deep down, you know what that is."

Doc stared at her, puzzled. She turned and walked toward the door. Before she went in, she paused with her hand on the knob. She looked back at him for a long moment. The corners of her eyes crinkled and a smile grew on her lips. "Doc, the answer is simple. Very, very simple." She nodded resolutely. "Just have faith." With that, she turned and vanished into the darkness of the house, the screen door banging shut behind her.

****

He tried to forget her. He taught his classes and tried to stay busy with his students so his thoughts would have other places to dwell besides lingering on her. Granny was right. He knew she was, but deep down he still struggled. Having faith was fine, but he felt a strong need to do *something* to solve the problem. He was never one who could escape into what he saw as denial and do nothing. He always believed that the Lord helps those who help themselves. Faith like Granny meant had always been a struggle for him.

The idea of Hadleigh going back to New York—a place he abhorred well before all this happened—and working with the same people who tried to harm her was horrifying to him. He loved her, wanted her, and now he feared for her.

Again and again he tried to bury himself in his work and his students, but his mind wouldn't rest. It was as though a compulsion he had never felt before had taken over his mind. And it would not be stilled.

"Doc? Er... I mean Sir?" Nathan interrupted his reverie, and Doc realized all his students were staring at him.

"What? Yes?" He tried desperately to pull himself back to reality.

"You said you were going to pick who would help you close up today."

"Oh! Yes. Of course." He looked out over the rows of expectant faces, waiting for the daily honor of helping him straighten up the room and bring in the next day's firewood. He tried to remember which student had proven to be the most deserving today, but his mind was a blank. He began shuffling items around on his desk, trying to bring to mind the most deserving pupil—trying to be fair. It was no use.

"Nathan, I'm going to ask you to stay today."

Muffled groans sounded, and Doc looked at them sternly. "Class dismissed." He hated being at a loss like that, but he had to make a choice. He watched them all file out of the building, and through the window he could see Nathan as he began gathering an armload of wood from the pile.

Suddenly he slammed his fist down on the desk. *I can't stand it! I have to try one more time to convince her. I'll show her some of my stamps before I sell them. Maybe that will help show her the truth. Maybe a tangible thing like that will be the key to her belief. I'll even take her to the dealer with me so she can see for herself the astonishment he always shows when I produce my samples. Yes! This might actually work!*

Doc glanced up and realized Nathan had returned and was standing by the stove, having just deposited his load of wood. He cocked his head and looked at Doc. "You leaving again?" Nathan asked, knowing the answer.

"Yes. But I should be back before classes start again on Monday. Can you finish up here for me?"

He shrugged. "Sure." Doc was already halfway out the door.

Chapter Eleven

Hadleigh returned to New York and the new rehearsal season. Success or failure, the regular contract period continued, and on that first morning back, Hadleigh stood before the bulletin board where the new cast list was posted. She hoped that now she would move up in the ranks and begin doing some principal roles, but she was disappointed. The reality stared back at her, in stark black and white print. Hadleigh was listed doing the same corps de ballet parts that she had always performed. Disappointment welled in her. She knew that Jasmine had a hand in this, and had influenced— probably insisted—that Adam not change the status quo. Apparently, she hadn't had enough of a scare after all. Hadleigh stared at the floor and sighed. It was now clear. There would never be a chance for her to progress here. She could accept it or move on.

Jann appeared beside her.

"You know why, of course." She put her arm around Hadleigh sympathetically.

Hadleigh nodded.

"You're not going to leave, are you?" Jann's expression clouded.

"I don't know. Where would I go?" She shrugged in resignation. "I hate the idea of attending any more cattle call auditions. They're so inhuman." Jann suppressed a slight smile at that last comment. Hadleigh didn't notice, she just picked her bag up off the floor and slung it over her shoulder. "What a mess."

"You could just stay here. Dancing is dancing, no matter what part you have. You always said it was the dancing you loved, not the fame and glory."

"Did I say that?" Hadleigh retorted with uncharacteristic sarcasm. "I must have been delusional."

"No, you just hadn't had the fame and glory yet, so you didn't know what you were missing. All those men—so little time—and so much adulation!" Jann feigned a swoon.

Hadleigh shoved her into the studio, her mood lightening despite everything. "Come on, duty calls. No matter what the circumstances, class must go on!" In spite of the casting board, it felt good to be home with Jann, and in blessedly familiar surroundings. The events of the past week were, thankfully, beginning to fade like a bad dream. She sighed. She would have plenty of time to think about what she needed to do with her future. Right now, she decided to bury her thoughts in the soothing repetition of pliés and tendus. Her beloved dancing—it was always there. Class, with its hypnotic progression, provided a complete and dependable escape. It never failed her. It was the one thing in life that could be counted on.

Halfway through barre, the idea took shape. Hadleigh had always noticed there was something inspirational about the physicality and repetition of class that seemed to produce a particular clear-headedness—like the fog peeling away on those allergy commercials. Before she finished the rond de jamb en l'air combination, she knew with a sure clarity what she must do. She would go back to the Cove, and try walking up the mountain through the cave route. It might just work for her, even if he wasn't with her. Perhaps, just perhaps, her love and desire would be enough to make the transition happen. After all, didn't something like that work in the movie *Brigadoon*? She knew the idea was irrational, but with a certainty she had never felt before in her life, she knew she had to try. There had to be some way for her to reach him, to find him and let him know that she was a fool not to have believed him when he had never given her any reason to doubt his sincerity. She would find a way—*somehow*—to let him know. She would start by trying to return to his world.

She also realized with a start that she didn't care if she left everything behind. The life she had been so satisfied with didn't seem to be of much value now. She loved her dancing, and always would. But she loved him more. She had to try and find him. If it meant sacrificing her job—so be it. After all, it wasn't looking especially promising at the moment, and it was obvious Adam was more interested in assuaging his wife than managing the company. There were other dance jobs, other companies. She wouldn't be giving up dancing altogether, just her current job. Despite what she had said to Jann about "cattle calls." she would go through them again, and gladly, if it was a part of her new life with Doc. Or not. Sometimes she wasn't sure, especially after the events at the competition, if she still wanted to have any part of the crazy performing world. She knew she wasn't quite thinking rationally, but she didn't care. She was past caring. She had to act, and act now.

So, long before the class ended, she made up her mind, and formulated her plan. She knew it was irrevocable and there would be no turning back and no second chances. Second chances were few and far between in the competitive dance world.

She briefly considered talking it all over with Jann but almost immediately decided against it. She'd have to reveal the truth about Doc and the Cove, and Jann would think Hadleigh had lost her mind. No, she couldn't tell Jann—as much as she wanted to share everything that had happened with her.

"Hey, you want to go grab something sinful for

lunch? Like donuts and a chili dog, or something equally creepy? I'm starving, and our rehearsal isn't scheduled until mid-afternoon." Jann caught her arm. "Come on...it'll do you good to put some junk food in your system. I hear it's good for whatever ails you. Clinical studies have shown..." she poked Hadleigh in the ribs. "What do you say?"

Hadleigh hesitated, appreciating Jann's attempt to lighten her mood and distract her. "Well..." she straightened her shoulders, "...noo, I think I'll stay here for a bit." Then she added apologetically, "I'll catch up with you later." Her voice almost caught, but she couldn't let Jann suspect what she was up to.

"Are you sure you're okay?" Jann was suspicious, noticing Hadleigh's fidgeting fingers.

Hadleigh avoided her stare and pasted a smile onto her face. "I'm fine. Please don't worry about me. I just need a little alone time, that's all." She gently pushed Jann down the hall. "Go on! Eat something rich and decadent for me."

Jann hesitated, sensing something amiss. But Hadleigh just raised her eyebrows at her, so Jann backed off and said, "Well, okay. But I'll be expecting a decent explanation later. And it better be good!"

Hadleigh murmured, "Thanks," picturing Jann's jaw dropping if she knew how "good" her explanation would be. Good, but unfortunately, unbelievable. She watched Jann wave her way out the door.

Then she waited. Less than patiently, she watched each dancer leave the building heading for lunch. It seemed to Hadleigh they were all taking their sweet time about it, but finally the building cleared out. Only then did she return to the dressing room to begin methodically packing up her belongings. There wasn't much to collect since Hadleigh never left much lying around except a few extra pairs of pointe shoes. These she picked up and stowed in her bag. She paused and took one last look around, zipped up her bag and walked purposefully down the hall. Hesitating only a moment, she took a deep breath and knocked on the door to Adam's office.

****

Hadleigh ran down the tracks as fast as she dared. She simply had to find him—to tell him everything, especially how sorry she was that she hadn't trusted him. It was just after dawn, and the dew still glistened on the grass. The morning mist hung low across the tracks, partially obscuring her vision. She had taken the earliest plane she could get, a red-eye, desperately hoping her plan would work.

A half hour later she reached the curve in the tracks, turned right, and began climbing up the trail, past the graffiti rock, ignoring her labored breathing. The mist grew heavier as she ascended, and when she arrived at the cave, she hesitated. Would her crazy idea really work? Would the transfer happen if he wasn't with her—just because of her intense desire? Would sheer willpower be enough to make the leap happen? *Well, I've come all this way, it simply has to work!* She made her way on into the cave, shivering in its coolness, but there was no electrical sensation this time. The goose bumps on her arm were because of the cold. She continued on out of the cave, still climbing, still hoping—until she finally broke out of the trees and onto the level road into the Cove.

It was quiet. Too quiet. The mist was just beginning to burn off, the warmth of the morning sun forcing its retreat. She slowed her gait a bit and strained to see through the fog. Would he be here? Did she succeed in getting into his time? She squinted her eyes to see through the haze. The tall shadowy silhouette of Granny's chimney came into view, and Hadleigh froze, a sick feeling punching its way into her stomach. That's all there was. Just a chimney, with the rubble of the cabin scattered below it. It was clear the house had burned long ago. Her hand flew to her throat as the full force of the truth slammed into her. She hadn't made it into his time period after all. She was in the Cove *today.*

She fought the urge to turn around and run back down the mountain. Her curiosity won out and she started walking again. Was everything gone? Hadleigh quickened her steps, and hurried down the road. She was anxious to see if anything at all was left of the town. To her relief, the schoolhouse bell tower became visible over the trees when she rounded the bend. Then her heart sank. As she approached it, she could see that the once pristinely painted structure was now weathered down to bare wood, and the glass in the two windows was long gone. She sighed. At least it was still standing and appeared to be reasonably watertight.

She slowed her pace as she came nearer, her gaze rising to the small bell tower. Although hard to make out, she thought she could still see the shadow of the bell Doc rang every morning to summon his students.

She hesitated for a moment at the foot of the steps, then stepped over the missing treads and pushed the door open. It gave no resistance at all, and the graffiti on it and the walls bore witness to the many hikers who had sought refuge here. The familiar black stove still squatted possessively in the middle of the room, although its rusted and deteriorating stack appeared to be balancing on the verge of collapse. Remnants of a few desks were scattered about, covered with a heavy coating of dust and dirt. The floor was caked with grime too, except where the hikers had left their footprints in it.

As her eyes adjusted more fully to the gloom of the interior, Hadleigh could see that, although the graffiti artists had almost completely covered the interior, they had—inexplicably—spared the blackboard. *That's odd.* She walked closer. Why such regard for that one area? Then she saw why. They had carefully avoided it in order to preserve the faint chalk writing still visible on the board, commemorating the last days of school. *So, they weren't such a destructive pack of animals after all.* She moved closer to read the writing. The day's tasks and pages assigned could still be made out in the top left hand corner, and—Hadleigh stopped cold and rubbed her eyes. She gave a small gasp, her hand flying to her mouth in amazement. There, faded but unmistakable, was written:

School closed forever in Hidden Cove, June 16, 1967
Doctor Collins, teacher

She reached out tentatively, barely touching her fingertips to the board. Her eyes filled with tears. It was Doc's handwriting! Slightly shaky—but definitely Doc's, no doubt about that—she had seen enough samples of it. So he was here in 1967, still alive, still teaching! She wrinkled her brow, and did a quick mental calculation...he would have been eighty-five years old!

Her mind raced. Did he close the school because he retired? Was he in poor health? Or was he forced to close it down for some other reason? She stood staring, mesmerized by the faded writing, and the most haunting question of all taunted her consciousness. Was she here, too? She hardly dared to think...or did he return here to marry someone else and raise a family...with lots of children... *grandchildren*, even?

Her heart pounding, she gazed around the room, studying its details, from floor to ceiling. She wasn't sure what she was looking for. She just wanted to find something, *anything* that might provide a clue to the specifics of Doc's long life here. And *her* life here, if she had had one. But the room held onto its secrets.

She walked back over to the blackboard, lightly caressing the board beneath the words one last time. Then she turned away and walked quickly out of the building.

Hadleigh meandered through the rest of the town—the little that was left of it. There were a few small outbuildings, a rusted old truck—*how had they ever managed to get that thing up here?* She found only two houses that hadn't yet succumbed to the elements. Like the schoolhouse, they were weathered down to bare wood, and it wouldn't be long before they, too, faded into history. Hadleigh assumed they must have been built later, or perhaps just better. She picked her way gingerly onto the porch of the larger one, stepping carefully across rotted and missing boards, and sat down on an old bench to rest, beat back her disappointment, and collect her churning thoughts.

Was it just not meant to be—a life with Doc? Had he come to the hospital on the day of her birth because he always kept the memory of her in his heart, based only on the few months they had together? The night she heard Pat's story, she had been so sure that it must have meant something else—that she been blessed with the gift of knowing the end of their story—and it was a happy one. One that indicated they had had a life together. But as she looked around her, that idea was dying fast.

She knew now and with a horrible clarity, there was no way for her to contact him. Her only hope was to have faith that someday he would try to find her again, and they could start over. She looked back down the road, past what was left of the little town. The mist was almost gone now, and she could see more detail through the trees. Her eyes focused in the distance, and she noticed, up on the rise of the hill, a small cemetery. Why hadn't she noticed it before? Because it had been shrouded by the heavy mist? She stared at it, and the idea took tangible shape. She grew cold. As if in a trance, she rose and began walking toward it, fear mixing with curiosity. Would she find him there? Did she really want to? She already knew he lived to be at least eighty-five. Could she handle any more information? What would she gain by it? Yet her feet kept moving toward the hill. Then she stopped abruptly, her hand flying to her constricting throat. What other marker might she find? Her heart pounded and she began to shake. Could she face the possibility of finding her own—and was it even possible? Her knees buckled, and she collapsed to the ground.

Chapter Twelve

Doc arrived in New York on a blustery, rainy, gray day. He hadn't thought to take his coat, so he was not only wet, but cold and wet. But he was used to extreme weather, so he just braced himself against the wind and made his way as fast as he could through the dampness to the Imperial Company's studios. Forcing the door open against the wind, he almost collided with Jann.

Her eyes widened. "I don't believe it." She shook her head. "Your timing couldn't be worse! If you're looking for Hadleigh—and of course you are—she's not here. She spoke to Adam right before lunch. She's resigned. I had the silly idea that she was now probably with you. But I can see...."

"She's not here? How long has she been gone? Didn't she say anything? Are you sure she's okay?" His mind spinning, he began to think the worst.

Jann's face clouded. "I thought she'd tell me before doing something like rash like this... but then, I should have realized something was up when she didn't want to go have lunch with me. I tried to call her at the apartment, but either she isn't there, or she isn't answering the phone. I was just getting ready to go over and check on her.

"Wouldn't she have told you where she was going or what she was planning to do? Someone couldn't have—coerced her into turning in her resignation, could they?"

"I don't think so." she cocked her head raised her eyebrows. "I think it may have had something to do with *you.*"

Doc looked at her, his jaw tensing. "I think this

whole thing smells like trouble. Surely, she would have said something to you if she had planned to leave the company for good. It just doesn't sound like her."

Jann nodded. "You're right about it being out of character for her, but she might not have confided in me, especially if it had anything to do with you. There's a lot she seems secretive about when it comes to that subject, and that is out of character for her, too." She bit her lip and looked up at him, concerned. "I know she was really disappointed when the cast list for our next season was posted," she paused for a moment before continuing, "but I still feel that's only part of it." She looked at him intently. "You know what I'm becoming more and more sure of? I think she's off trying to find you." She met his eyes and added, "Would she know where to look?"

Doc nodded. "Sort of. But she can't do it. Not without...." he stopped, realizing that Jann apparently knew little about the details of Hadleigh's visit to the Cove.

Jann continued on. "Look, I know there's some big mystery here that she didn't want to talk about. I'll admit that has always really intrigued me. Hadleigh usually doesn't have secrets. She's always open and honest. That's why I think her sudden resignation has more to do with you than the company situation. Is it possible that this—mystery—might have anything to do with her sudden decision?"

Doc nodded, a chill worse than the wet outdoors descending on him. "But if that's what she's done, I need to stop her before...." he hesitated, "...before she gets there..." he finished with a sigh. If she had indeed gone back to the Cove, she would find it as it exists *today*, at this exact moment. There was no way she could use the portal to get back into his time, and the Cove in today's world he knew nothing

163

about. He had always avoided it—deliberately. It would be almost a sacrilege for him to go there and see what it had become, or what was left. Or, *who* was left. He didn't even know if it was possible for him to do it, and it was something he didn't care to find out.

He turned his attention back to Jann. "Are you sure that there isn't any other explanation? Could she have gone back to stay with Pat?"

Jann paused for a moment, considering that possibility. Then she rejected it, shaking her head. "I know she was disappointed in the recent casting, and she was feeling pretty discouraged, but if she had decided to go back home, I'm sure she would have said something to me. Nothing about this makes sense. It's not like her, " she looked at Doc almost accusingly, "but then, when it comes to you, anything is possible with her, and it wouldn't surprise me if she suddenly decided to track you down and just acted on that impulse. Very uncharacteristic of her, but not impossible," she said, her eyes narrowing, "under the circumstances."

Doc put his hands on her shoulders. "But you're certain she didn't go somewhere else? To another company? You're absolutely certain someone didn't try to manipulate—or hurt her again?"

Jann felt his hands shaking. "No, I'm not sure. But I think the peanut incident was entirely related to the competition—not something that would happen here. And Hadleigh would never allow herself to be manipulated. If she'd had an offer from another company, I'm sure she would have discussed it with me. And I don't think anyone has, or would...well, I just think she is probably looking for you." She stripped off her pointe shoes. "Look, let's go back to my apartment on the off chance that she might still be there, and if not, we can look around and see if she left any indication about what she's up to. I didn't do that this morning because I assumed she'd left earlier than I—not unusual—and then she was here, and seemed to be completely normal, except for being a little sad and disappointed, which was understandable." She headed back toward the dressing rooms, calling over her shoulder, "I'll be out in just a minute."

Doc paced back and forth, his fear mounting. How could Jann be so sure nothing was wrong? The terrible sick feeling in the pit of his stomach was growing by the second. Oh, he'd love to think that she'd suddenly had a change of heart and had come looking for him, but it didn't make sense. She had been so certain he was delusional, and understandably so. She was so stubborn and independent about it that he was convinced the only answer was that someone had tried again to hurt or coerce her, and succeeded. This whole thing was so out of character for Hadleigh—Jann all but admitted as much. Why would she suddenly decide to come and find him? Did she just, out of the blue, start believing him? That didn't make sense at all. None of it made any sense.

****

They arrived, breathless and shivering, at the apartment, and Jann began to go through each room. Looking for evidence, she called it, and she didn't have to look far. Almost immediately, she found the note. It was placed neatly in an envelope propped up by a coffee cup on the kitchen table. Jann ripped it open and began reading.

"I know you're going to think I'm crazy, and you are probably also going to be upset that I didn't tell you any of this before class today. Well, that was because I didn't know any of this before class. It just suddenly became clear to me that I no longer belong at Imperial. I had to act on that right away, before I lost my nerve. The time to resign is now—at the beginning of the new season—before rehearsals start. I didn't want to disrupt things any more than

necessary. I didn't say anything to you because I just made up my mind during class, and frankly, I didn't want you to try and talk me out of it. You have to know I can't stay here. There's no future in it for me, and I have to do what I must. I will be back soon to collect my things and decide what my next step (no pun intended—don't you dare smile) will be. The worst part is not working with you anymore. You are my best friend in the world, and I will miss you terribly. But I know that you, better than anyone, will understand what I have done and what I have to do. I'll be in touch soon. Please don't worry about me.

Hadleigh."

Jann looked up and said matter-of-factly, "See? She *has* gone to look for you."

Doc looked surprised. "She didn't say that."

"It's what she didn't say. She didn't say where she was going, and if it was as simple as going home to Pat, she would have said so. But she didn't. So, she's off looking for you, just like I suspected."

Doc's mind began racing. "If that's true, then I don't have any time to waste. I have to find her, and stop her, before she...." he struggled for the right words, "...does what I think she's going to try to do. I have to stop her!" Doc was already halfway to the door, but he stopped mid-step and turned to face her.

"When she comes back here, and I pray that she will—tell her I was here. Let her know I came to find her, to tell her..." he hesitated, trying to find the right words, trying to formulate a Plan B. "...tell her I will come back here, soon, I'm just not sure exactly when I'll be able to get away. But I *will* return to her. Tell her to please, please stay here and wait for me."

Jann nodded. "Just promise me you'll both finally tell me what this whole thing is all about, okay? This mysterious cat-and-mouse business is about to drive me crazy!" She smiled and held the door for him. "Good luck! I'm afraid you're going to need it."

Shaking her head, she watched him until he vanished down the stairs. Jann was becoming more and more curious about this man and his mysterious hold on her friend. She had no doubt that he cared for her—apparently very deeply. That was evident in his eyes and his body language. He had trembled just speaking her name. Jann fervently hoped that Hadleigh hadn't acted too impulsively and gotten herself into trouble or a situation she wouldn't be able to back out of. She knew the dance company would never take her back, even if she had a change of heart, but judging by Doc's reaction that might be the least of her worries. She sighed. This whole thing was so unlike her. She wished Hadleigh had confided in her about Doc's secret. It must be a doozy. She smiled to herself, in spite of everything. She knew she'd find out eventually, since Hadleigh had written that she would be back to pick up her things. So when she returned, Jann would demand that she come clean with her. Jann was certain she would—she'd just have to be patient and cool her jets until then.

****

Doc arrived at the airport ticket counter in record time. "When's the next flight to Johnson City, Tennessee? I don't care where the connection is, I just need the one that will arrive the soonest." He dug into his pockets.

The agent barely looked up from her computer. "I'm sorry, sir, but the Johnson City airport is closed right now—" the tic tic tic of her fingernails on the keyboard barely slowed, "—due to a security issue." She looked up at him. "But I can get you on a late flight connecting in Charlotte to Asheville. Will that do?"

He nodded. "I guess it will have to. When does it leave?"

She consulted her screen. "Late. Ten twenty-five

tonight, arriving in Asheville at four-forty am, with a two hour layover in Charlotte."

Sighing in resignation, he said, "I'll take it." He counted out the money and placed in on the counter. *Thank goodness I sold that extra set of stamps last time.* He handing over almost every bit of cash he had. When he had time, he usually took the bus, but...He checked his watch and groaned. It was barely two pm. It was going to be a long, anxious wait. Then there was the problem of getting from the Asheville airport up into the mountains. Well, he'd just have to hitchhike and hope for the best.

What would happen if Hadleigh got to the Cove? What would she find? More importantly, how would it affect her? She had just given up her job—a job he knew she loved and worked most of her life for—obviously convinced that she would be able to find him. What had suddenly changed her mind? Some altercation between her and Jasmine? What would she do if she got there and realized...what? That he wasn't there—or that the whole town wasn't there? He had no idea what she would find. Whatever she found was certain to be a shock and not what she expected. Although—he almost smiled at the thought—it would probably go a long way toward convincing her of the complete truth of his story.

He came back to reality with a start when the woman in line behind him cleared her throat more loudly than necessary. Apologizing, Doc moved away and settled himself uncomfortably in a vinyl chair across from the ticket counter.

He lost track of time for a while, then suddenly, the voice of the ticket agent cut through his wandering thoughts. "Sir? Sir?" He looked up, and she motioned him back up to the counter.

"I have one seat open on a flight leaving in fifteen minutes—interested?"

"Absolutely!" Then he stopped, his heart sinking. "How much more?"

"Actually, it's twenty-five dollars less. But you better hurry!" She handed him his change and his boarding pass, and he sprinted off toward the gate.

Chapter Thirteen

Hadleigh continued to sit there, ignoring the damp ground, her forehead resting on her knees. For a long time she stayed there, her eyes closed, until the moisture saturated her jeans and she began to shiver. Finally making up her mind, knowing she was accomplishing nothing by sitting there except getting soggy, she rose and straightened her shoulders. She brushed herself off. Hesitating only a moment, she walked up the small hill and pushed at the protesting metal gate. She gave it another push and noticed it had been cleverly fashioned out of an old metal bedstead. Waste not, want not, was definitely one of the unspoken rules in the Cove. She gave it one final shove, and it creaked open just wide enough to let her slide through.

The cemetery, unlike the adjoining community, appeared to be somewhat maintained. Although not exactly manicured, it wasn't completely overgrown, and most of the markers were cleared of weeds. There was also an odd feature Hadleigh had never seen before. Some graves were covered by what looked like small wooden houses. Was this a custom of his Melungeon people? She wondered. She'd have to remember to ask him about that. Then she winced. That is, if she ever saw him again.

Determined now, she read every legible marker. There weren't many—less than ten or fifteen. She soon realized there were no names she recognized. But then, she had never been formally introduced to anyone in the cove except Nathan and Granny—Myrtle—she remembered, and she didn't even know if her last name was the same as Doc's. There was no Myrtle, or Nathan, for that matter, and blessedly, no Doc...or...She sighed, relieved and disappointed at the same time. If she and Doc had made a life here, she should have found one or both of them. But there was nothing.

Confused, tired, and not knowing what to do next, Hadleigh walked back down the hill toward the town. She stopped at Granny's chimney and ran her hands slowly over the darkened bricks. It wasn't so long ago that she and Doc sat here, enjoying those huge sandwiches. It all seemed like a dream—more so now in this haunted setting. And, she thought wryly, a dream she had just given up her job for. Whatever had possessed her? She was supposed to be stable and practical. She was the dependable one who always reigned in her friends when they started to do something crazy or imprudent. She should have talked to Jann, or someone, before making such a rash decision. Oh, Adam had tried to talk her out of it, but she was too stubborn to listen. Now here she was, with nothing and nowhere to go. She could go back home to Aunt Pat. She could go back to her apartment, and try to explain to Jann the reasoning behind this most depressing turn of events. What a nightmare! The whole situation was made even worse because it was of her own doing. There was no one else to blame. Well, Aunt Pat often said she was her own worst enemy, and of course she was right. Hadleigh hated to admit defeat and come crawling home, although she knew would be welcomed with open arms, and with plenty of advice on what to do about the rest of her life. She certainly needed that now! She had been so sure she would find him here, and that love would conquer all. *So much for romantic fantasies. Well, from now on, practicality will rule.*

After walking aimlessly about, she found herself back at the larger house with the big porch and went inside. As her eyes adjusted to the dark interior, she could see that, once again, the walls and even the ceilings were covered with graffiti—lots of it. Apparently, local hikers missed no opportunity to record their names and exploits—but, she decided charitably, they *had* spared the writing on the blackboard. She continued to wander slowly through the rooms, careful to avoid places where the floor had rotted away. There wasn't much to see. There was a large iron headboard, like the one at the cemetery, rusting away against one wall, and a few broken pieces of china scattered on the floor. Everything else must have been carried off years ago.

She knew she was stalling, not wanting to go back down the mountain and get herself on a flight back to the city, as if by lingering she could will Doc to suddenly appear. She knew better, and she also knew that she really didn't want to get caught up here after dark. She glanced at her watch—she should get moving. Darkness came early here, with the light fading immediately when the sun dipped below the mountaintops. Nevertheless, she continued to move deeper into the house. She found two small bedrooms, completely empty except for dust balls and the omnipresent coating of dirt. She kept willing herself to leave, but instead she found herself drawn to a large room at the back of the house. A huge room, it was empty except for a single broken chair balanced at a remarkable angle in the corner. She wondered why the builder had provided such a big space. Most houses in the Cove were extremely small, often with only one bedroom, if that. This room was huge—by Cove standards—and even had several windows. This, too, was unusual for such a cold mountain climate.

She kicked absently at a dirt clump on the floor, trying to force herself to get on with it. With a sigh, she finally turned around to start her trek back down the mountain. But something caught her eye.

A flash of gold, briefly illuminated by a sunbeam shining through the wisps of dust. She walked closer. Had one of the hikers lost a piece of jewelry? Not likely, since she didn't think hikers would be wearing much jewelry. Whatever it was, it was stuck fast between the floorboards. Hadleigh bent down to dig it out. She poked at it, and it crumbled in her fingers, leaving them sticky.

It took a moment for it to register. Then Hadleigh gasped, and her heart raced. She knew very well what it was. She dug deeper, bringing up more—coating her fingers with it. Yes! It was rosin! Derek's "magic turnout powder"! There was only one way it could have gotten to this place, lodged stubbornly between the floorboards. She began scrutinizing the rest of the floor and found a few other places where her probing fingers found remnants of the sticky substance. That's when it all fell into place and she knew—absolutely—what this room had been used for, and built for. A dance studio! Her heart soared! *She did end up here*! Doc must have built this house, and with it, a large room she could use as a studio. And tiny bits of rosin—*her rosin*—had survived, wedged deeply in the floor!

Hadleigh ran out of the house, ecstatic. She knew now he would find her! She didn't know when, or how, but she had proof that it would happen—*had happened.*

She ran out through the remains of the town and toward the downhill trail. She wasn't tired anymore and had the energy of ten men, she was so happy. She flew down the trail, bypassing the cave route, ignoring the rocks and encroaching branches that attempted to slow her descent. She blazed through them all and arrived at the graffiti rock in record time. Out of breath, she dropped down onto it to rest.

As she collapsed on the cool granite and tried to calm her breathing, she gazed down toward the

Nolichucky River below. It was so beautiful and wild. The fog had long burned off now, revealing an expanse of undulating blue mountains beyond. She inhaled the damp woodsy smell of the forest and heard, far below her, the rush of the river. Her attention then wandered down to the tracks that hugged the cliffs as they wound off far, far into the distance.

That's when she saw him. She blinked, not believing her eyes. It was so distant she found it difficult to focus. She blinked again, scarcely daring to hope—but it truly was Doc! He seemed panicked—staring straight ahead and walking in long, fast strides. His bag slung over his shoulder, he made his way around the far curve in the tracks just visible on the horizon and began his climb up the long, narrow incline of the tracks toward her.

Hadleigh stood up on the rock, and at that moment, distant as she was, he saw her. He paused only momentarily, then dropped his bag and ran. She was already running down the rock, down the trail, and onto the tracks toward him, closing the long mile between them as fast as she could. She ran frantically, half stumbling over gravel and the railroad ties, never taking her eyes off him. The tracks had never seemed this long before! They seemed to grow maddeningly with every step she took. Her heart pounded, and she felt like her lungs were about to burst—and still he seemed so far away. But finally—*finally*—the long distance closed between them, and she felt herself being gathered into his warm, strong arms. She melted into his embrace, both of them breathing hard and fast. So winded neither of them could speak, Doc removed his arms from around her and took her hand, bringing it to his face and pressing his kiss against it. Then, looking at her with an expression of mixed wonderment and joy, he squeezed it three times. And Hadleigh knew she had, at last, come home.

Epilogue

His feet spread apart; he stood braced against the wind, hair whipping around his face. He watched the fine gray powder as it whirled around and up and away. Caught in the currents of air, it separated into wisps of smoky ribbon, spiraling and dancing, spiraling and dancing, out—further and further, over the mountaintop. *How appropriate*, he thought.

She always said if she died first, she wanted to be cremated. This was important to her, despite its going against long-standing Cove traditions. And no marker, either, she insisted. She did not want to have her life commemorated in that way.

She also asked that he scatter her ashes from the hill at the top of the Cove, near the schoolhouse. It was her sacred place, where she first heard the truth about his life. The truth she hadn't believed. It was where she had come close to making a decision that would have robbed her of this life she loved— the life she shared with him. She assured him that by honoring her wishes, she would always be a part of his world.

He did as she requested. He understood why.

Only a few years later, the town—for all intents and purposes—ceased to exist. The inhabitants didn't recognize it then, of course, and they all said they'd be back. Back just as soon as the state gave them money again for a school, so the children didn't have to travel so far away just to attend the city school.

So, pulling away one at a time, all the families soon moved down, down into the world they had sought so hard to avoid, all for the sake of the children. They left quickly but reluctantly, leaving many of their possessions behind. After all, they assured themselves, they'd be back soon. As soon as humanly possible.

The days turned into weeks, the weeks into months. Quietly the years passed, and the Cove became more or less forgotten. Doc had his stroke soon after fighting his family's move down off the mountain, and Nathan had regretfully placed him in The Center until he could, Nathan hoped, completely recover. Doc hated it, hated everything about it, and had no intention of staying a minute longer than he had to. So he worked hard at his rehab, but was careful to hide from the staff the true level of his recovery. He didn't want them to stop him from carrying out his plan. The plan he and she had agreed upon so many years before. His plan to visit the hospital—to see her one last time.

And so he set his plan to action—slowly and methodically. He left The Center just after midnight. It was so early in the new day it was easy to slip out without anyone noticing. It took him longer than he expected to get to her hospital, but he had allowed plenty of time.

It took him several minutes to find the right section, but when he did, no one stopped him or questioned his being there. He walked in short shuffling steps through the heavy double doors and found the window overlooking the nursery. Leaning on his cane, he stopped, his heart pounding. Only one bassinet was occupied, but he would have known her immediately even if the room had been filled to capacity. He stared, transfixed—and the tiny bundle seemed to blur and fade. He rubbed his eyes and blinked as the vision grew into focus. His beautiful Hadleigh! She looked as real and palpable as always. He watched her, happiness flowing into his soul again. Her image danced before him, and he reached for her.

His hand slammed against the barrier of cold glass. Absolute and unchangeable, like the time that separated them. Hot tears burned their way to the surface and spilled down his face. He couldn't take his eyes off her, and he was afraid he wouldn't be able to make himself leave. So he just stood there, his legs shaking.

Suddenly he sensed someone staring at him. He forced his attention away from the window and saw a woman approaching, her expression questioning. Abruptly he turned away and walked back through the double doors. He'd already stayed much longer than he'd planned, and he had to make it to the mountain and into the Cove before dark.

It was late—much later than he had calculated when he finally walked out of the hospital. He hailed another taxi and traveled off into the morning light, far away from the glare of the rising sun, relieved at last to be riding away forever from the stifling "town people."

The taxi finally groaned to a halt at the end of the dirt road, and the driver climbed out to help him. He got out slowly and paid the man his money. The driver hesitated.

"Don't you want me to wait?"

"No, thank you. My friend will be meeting me here shortly." He waved a crooked hand impatiently in his direction. "Go on, now. I'll be perfectly alright. Go on about your business."

Hesitating a moment more, he finally shrugged, folded his long legs back into the driver's seat, and disappeared in a cloud of dust. Doc watched until the brake lights vanished around the bend, and then waited until every speck of dust had died back onto the road. Only then did he take a good look around.

The depot looked almost the same. But slowly gathering clouds had begun to darken the sky, so he couldn't see that portions of the roof had long since fallen in and the benches inside now served as squirrel highways. The big difference he did notice was the silence. It was the kind of silence that either embraced or oppressed, depending on one's frame of mind. It had *never* been that silent here. Up in the Cove, yes. But never here. Here it had been loud, constantly changing, and exciting. People hurrying or lingering, tears mixing with dust on their faces when they kissed loved ones hello or goodbye. The hot smell of the trains was missing, too. He paused. Was he confusing fact with fantasy? He shook his head in an effort to clear it. Sometimes it was hard to remember. Sometimes hard to forget. He took a deep breath and drew in the heady scent of decaying leaves mixed with the musty nostalgia of the station itself. It restored him.

He leaned heavily on his cane and looked down the tracks. He always found it fascinating— railroads, roads, or paths—anything that grew ever smaller while meandering out of sight. He always wanted to know—what lay around the far corner? What adventures might he find? What secrets? Ah, yes. Well, he had become somewhat of a romantic in his older years. More like her. He smiled.

But these tracks were particularly good material for flights of imagination. On the left, those old familiar rock cliffs rose up dramatically, almost completely vertical, with only a narrow space between the tracks and the rock itself. His gaze traveled to the other side, with its short piece of level ground, and its sudden drop into the Nolichucky gorge, it's long shimmer of river coursing eternally far below.

He took one final look around. Then, leaning on his cane, he began walking, one methodical, shuffling step at a time, down the tracks.

It took him a long time to get there. Most of the time he spent getting up the mountain, even though it was only a half mile. He had to stop often to rest, but he was determined, and he made steady, if slow, progress. But the storm clouds continued gathering ominously in the west, and soon the forest trail was almost completely dark. The low rumbles and flashes of light grew closer and more insistent. Doc tried to pick up his pace.

He managed to emerge onto the level ground of the Cove before any rain began, but by the time he reached Granny's old homeplace, he was buffeted by the wind, exhausted, and shivering. It was setting up to be quite a storm—probably a regular "frog strangler," as Granny used to say. He smiled at the childhood memory in spite of the chill that had settled immediately to his bones.

The wind at his back pushed him through the door and into the relative safety of the house. He shook himself off, running his hands through his hair in an attempt to get it out of his face. Immediately, calmness coursed through him. He felt better and more at peace than he had in months, despite the increasing howl of the wind. He knew this was where he needed to be. *Home.* It was worth all the effort to get here—back where he *had* to be.

Before he gave into his body's cries for rest, he needed to muster the strength to get a fire started. He was chilled to the bone and finding it increasingly difficult to move. So, despite his protesting limbs, he braced himself against the wind and limped outside. He worked his way to the side of the cabin where he always stored a supply of wood. There was little left to choose from, but it would have to do.

He grabbed all he had the energy to carry and made his way back into the house. He dropped the wood on the dirt-covered hearth and began to work through the steps of building a fire. It was second nature to him, and he soon coaxed the initial flickers into a large blaze. Exhausted, he leaned against the mantel and allowed the warmth to course through him.

Suddenly, the familiar hot pain hit his chest, and his vision clouded. He clutched at the edge of the fireplace to keep from collapsing. He hung on, waiting for it to pass, but it seemed worse this time, and it was taking longer for it to ease. He knew he couldn't stay downstairs any longer, despite the warm fire. He had to be upstairs in his haven—the tiny garret room that had been his refuge since childhood. The fire's warmth would rise up there soon enough, he knew from experience. And he *had* to get up there, because the little loft space—his personal sanctuary—had been an important place for him throughout his life. He came here in contemplation, as well as in joy or sorrow. It was where he brought her after she vowed to spend the rest of her life with him. He remembered the mica window at the far end of the gable, under the eaves. Only a tiny opening, it gave such a wondrous, luminous light! It always reminded him of the big churches in her world, and it gave him a feeling of peace. He returned to this place often, even as an adult, and it felt right that he should return here now.

The pain subsided somewhat, and a slight smile came to his lips as another flash from his childhood rose in his mind. He remembered those nights spent at Granny's, wrapped in layers of her soft, well-worn quilts, gazing out the large window at the vast dark sky and its stars. Then he frowned. There would be no stars to see tonight. He shook his head to clear his thoughts of the past, and slowly, painfully, made his way over to the stairs. He climbed his way to the top, meticulously, two footsteps for each stair, stopping often to catch his breath. At last, crawling into the room at the top, he eased his body down and looked around. His eyes strained to find his favorite mica window—but found only an empty, gaping hole. The other window was gone, too, allowing much of the wind and chill to permeate, despite the deep overhang of the roof. The attic floor was coated with dust and dirt, but he didn't care. None of that mattered now. He pulled his body deeper under the eaves to a space where he could still watch the angry sky as it strained—shrieking and flashing futilely—without producing rain.

He tried to settle himself, but abruptly the pain returned, crushingly intense, and this time he could feel curtains of blackness curling behind his eyes. He closed them and collapsed all the way down, pillowing his head on his arm.

He tried to block out the pain by calling up a picture of her in his mind, something he always did before drifting off to sleep. Even during all the years of their marriage, when she lay peacefully beside him, he liked to carry her image with him into sleep.

He focused his mind on her. Gradually, a deep, relaxing peace began coursing through his body. Like shedding a heavy layer of clothing, every muscle in his body relaxed. The pain stopped, so suddenly, so completely, it surprised him, and his eyes flew open. He expected to see the familiar dark outline of the ceiling eaves. Instead, he saw the vast night sky studded with stars—bright, brilliant stars all around him—amazing on such a stormy night.

He looked down and realized, without any sense of alarm, that he could see the cabin below him, smoke curling from the chimney. Then he saw something else, something every Cove resident lived in fear of, and yet he felt no concern whatsoever. Fire. A chimney fire. Fueled by the wind, it had already jumped to the roof, small pockets of flame weaving their determined way along the shingles. He watched, feeling only an interested detachment, as the fire increased and cabin receded further and further away from him.

He looked up, away from the disappearing cabin, his attention now drawn to an intense glow ahead of him. It was the most vivid light he had ever seen, yet it didn't hurt his eyes. He strained to see into the extraordinary brightness. Could it be? Hadleigh? His beautiful Hadleigh? Yes! It *was* Hadleigh! The light moved closer, and he saw her clearly. She seemed to be standing onstage, bathed in a vibrant spotlight. Her hair fell in soft tendrils around her face, and her chiffon costume flowed over her. She looked exactly as she had the first time he'd ever seen her perform. But this time the spotlight was different. It was brighter...much, much brighter. It was getting larger, coming closer. Like the mountain mist, it began to envelop him.

Then suddenly Hadleigh was before him, her arms outstretched, her expression radiant. She said nothing, but Doc understood it all in a heartbeat. Time, their constant obstacle, was gone. Never again would there be the dilemma of being in *his* time, or *her* time. Time, as they had always understood it, no longer existed. The barrier was swept away.

She reached for him, and he slipped his arm around her, pulling her close. Then, gazing into her upturned face, he traced two fingers slowly down her cheek.

About the Author

Violet Rightmire is the pen name of Debra Webb Rogers, a retired professional ballet dancer. She was born in Ithaca, New York, but lived most of her life in Florida. She graduated from Florida State University with a B.S. degree in Education, and currently teaches dance at Douglas Anderson School of the Arts in Jacksonville.

Ms. Webb was a dancer with The Birmingham Ballet, The Israel Ballet, and The Florida Ballet. She has been a guest artist and teacher at schools and companies throughout the southeast, and has appeared in *Bride's* magazine and in a commercial that won both an Addy and an Emmy award.

Ms. Webb has published two works of nonfiction: *The Boone Connection,* and *Dancing Between the Ears.* She has written for the national magazine *Dancebag,* and a guest column for the *Florida Times-Union. Dancing in Time* is her first novel.

When she is not teaching or writing, Ms. Webb enjoys hiking and exploring the Appalachian Mountains with her husband Sam.

Her website address is debrawebbrogers.com.

Thank you for purchasing this Wild Rose Press publication. For other wonderful stories of romance, please visit our on-line bookstore at www.thewildrosepress.com.

For questions or more information contact us at info@thewildrosepress.com.

The Wild Rose Press
www.TheWildRosePress.com

LaVergne, TN USA
21 August 2009
155532LV00001B/3/P